A TERROR FROM WITHIN

Larry E. Wooten

iUniverse, Inc.
New York Bloomington

A Terror from Within

This is a work of fiction. All of the characters, names, incidents,
organizations, and dialogue in this novel are either the products
of the author's imagination or are used fictitiously.

iUniverse books may be ordered through booksellers or by contacting:

iUniverse
1663 Liberty Drive
Bloomington, IN 47403
www.iuniverse.com
1-800-Authors (1-800-288-4677)

Because of the dynamic nature of the Internet, any Web addresses or links contained in this
book may have changed since publication and may no longer be valid. The views expressed
in this work are solely those of the author and do not necessarily reflect the views of the
publisher, and the publisher hereby disclaims any responsibility for them.

ISBN: 978-1-4401-9886-1 (pbk)
ISBN: 978-1-4401-9888-5 (cloth)
ISBN: 978-1-4401-9887-8 (ebook)

Printed in the United States of America

iUniverse rev. date: 1/11/10

Prologue

Yousef Khan focused assiduously on his task at hand. He busied himself pouring small quantities of ammonium nitrate into his blender. Once the small pill-like granules reached the consistency of a fine powder, Khan poured the pulverized concentrate into a 55 gallon plastic barrel. After months of this tedious effort, the container was finally filled. He carefully replaced the top of the drum ensuring that the barrel was as air tight as possible.

Khan's next undertaking was a bit more challenging and far more dangerous. He had obtained large glass jugs of acetone and hydrogen peroxide from a chemical supply outlet. He concentrated the peroxide liquid by heating small quantities then carefully combined the two distilled liquids while submersing into an ice bath to control the exothermic or self-heating reaction. This was a vital safety concern, according to the Jihadist manual he was utilizing. After several hours the distilled liquids were ready to be combined with the final ingredient of hydrochloric acid. He had purchased a Pyrex vessel to mix the chemicals. Again, utilizing an ice bath to control the exothermic reaction, he very slowly and deliberately made small batches of the "explosive" known as **Mother of Satan.** Over time, the small liquid batches produce a white crystalline powder much like sugar. Khan stored the powder in a refrigerator unit outside in his detached garage.

Next he purchased a (2.5 meters long by 20 centimeters in diameter) cast iron pipe from a plumbers supply store. He modified the pipe by welding a metal disk to close off one end. To the other end, he fashioned a detachable cone-shaped apparatus. Into the tip of the cone, Khan inserted a steel rod with rounded metal orbs screwed into each end. Finally he obtained his last container of nitro-methane fuel oil. This final bottle along with the previous 52, two-litter bottles had been bought from various model car racing supply stores. This had transpired over the last four months. At last acquiring all components to his device, Khan recited, "Insha'Allah" (God willing).

CHAPTER 1

MOHAMMAD KAZMI'S AND Ali Jawed's late model Ford rolled slowly to the shoulder of the unpaved road. Mohammad furtively exited the vehicle and fingered the "safety flare" as he searched for any human movement. Cautiously, he ignited the flare and placed it into a valley of dry brush. Quickly the thick undergrowth caught fire and continued downwind into the valley.

Mohammad quickly climbed back into the automobile while Ali drove watchfully towards their next destination. Within minutes they were on California U.S. highway 1. Mohammad studied his U.S. Forest Service map to best determine the next targeted area. Again, Ali departed the highway and found a deserted unpaved road. As before, Mohammad leaned into the back seat and pulled a flare from the first cardboard case of 72. Once more, Mohammad tore off the plastic cap from the flare exposing the striking surface which he rubbed against the cap to once again ignite the flare.

These efforts continued on throughout the hot and dry August day. Mohammad and Ali had almost 400 roadside emergency flares to employ. The plan was for all flares to be deployed by 12:00 o'clock noon the following day. Four additional teams with identical missions had been dispatched to Texas, New Mexico, Nevada, and Arizona. Their *Leader* had been explicit and detailed in assigning these tasks. All men had shaved any facial hair and had fresh hair cuts within the last two weeks. All were instructed to wear typical college student attire of jeans and tee-shirts. Additionally all men were directed to obey traffic laws and regulations, and finally to fit into the community that they traveled through.

Within hours of the first day, first responders consisting of local fire departments, local agents from the Bureau of Land Management, the National Park Service, and even various Native American Indian tribes were reacting to the numerous fires within their designated areas. By early evening, the local communities were overwhelmed. The U.S. Forest Service deployed its "Hotshot Crews" as emergency calls came in. Shortly, the Crews were besieged with additional breakouts. Emergency management teams from each state requested that their respective governor deploy National Guard personnel to help. By nightfall, the five western states were critically inundated with out-of-control fires. Federal officials requested that all available active duty military personnel be deployed to help out wherever they could.

Late evening on the first day, a night watch officer at the National Operations Center or NOC, located at the Nebraska Avenue Complex in Washington D.C, observed the uncontrolled burning from satellite coverage. In addition to news coverage with frenzied local officials, the watch officer noticed the blazing forest land, was limited to just five states. He wondered to himself, "Why would these states have out-of-control fires and not the adjacent states, like Colorado or Utah?" The watch officer called an emergency number for the National Meteorological Center at Camp Springs, Maryland. The operator connected him to the "operations desk." The NOC watch officer inquired as to the precipitation in the fire ravaged states along with bordering states like Colorado and Utah. The meteorological official ensured him that all the southwestern states were dry with limited rains forecasted. The watch officer pondered this response for some time as he hung up the phone. He then sought out the Senior Duty Officer. The watch officer explained to his "boss" that the fires devastating the western U.S. might have been deliberate acts of terrorism. After some deliberation, the senior official made a phone call to the FBI.

Within hours, the FBI stood up their Strategic Information Operations Center, more commonly known as SIOC. During a crisis, it functions as a nerve center of the FBI, providing analytical, logistic, and administrative support to the investigative teams on the ground. Along with FBI personnel, personnel from other federal agencies such as the Department of Homeland Security are represented.

CHAPTER 2

YOUSEF KHAN WAS born in Pakistan (*Land of the Pure*) in 1980. His father owned a Gold Souk (jewelry store) in Islamabad, and the family were devoted Muslims. Yousef was the first son. Although, he had two younger brothers and two younger sisters, he was favored by his mother for his calm demeanor. His father preferred Yousef, not only because he was the eldest son to one day take over the family business, but because of his studious, good-natured manner.

Yousef graduated from a Higher Secondary School with honors and asked his father if he could study abroad to obtain his university degree. His father was pleased with his son's request because it represented a special respect and admiration to the family for a progeny to be educated outside of Pakistan.

He used his father's work computer to research possible university options. His first choice was to apply to the University of Cambridge. Upon further reflection, he decided to investigate universities in the United States. When Yousef explored the "internet," he was intrigued by the huge land of so many cultures, varied religions, and wide open space.

One day when he was helping out in his father's store where he would occupy many hours "surfing the web," he came upon a website for the University of New Mexico, in Albuquerque. The university webpage was filled with information concerning major areas of study, climate, sports, and local sights. The more he searched, the more he became fascinated with the university, locale, and attractions. He was enthralled by the mountainous desert area that looked so much like Pakistan—but so much more. He was engrossed in the varied areas of university study. But more than anything he was awestruck with the local area sights like the balloon fiesta. He saw beautiful pictures of literally hundreds of hot-air balloons floating high above the city, which was nestled in the valley of tall mountains.

This was my destiny thought Yousef, "Insha'Allah," he muttered to himself. That very day he printed out an on-line University of New Mexico application.

Several weeks passed and he at last received confirmation that he had been admitted to the fall semester at the University of New Mexico. His family, especially his father, was ecstatic. Two weeks prior to the start of classes, Yousef boarded an airplane bound for the United States. He traveled from Pakistan to London, and then onto Los Angeles, California. After a four hour wait at LAX, he boarded a jet to his final destination, Albuquerque.

After collecting his bags at the Sunport Airport, he met up with his student guide in front of the airport. The guide, a Pakistani like Yousef, was a junior at the university majoring in engineering as Yousef intended to do. After a whirlwind tour of the campus, he was shown his room at student housing, where the upperclassman promised to escort Yousef to the freshman orientation early the next morning.

The diminutive Yousef, stood only 5 feet 4 inches tall. With his reticent manner, hooked nose, and a slight stammer, he found it difficult making friends and enjoying a social life. In the classroom, however, Yousef excelled. He received his bachelors' degree in mechanical engineering in three years, and was encouraged by the dean of engineering to continue his schooling and to apply for a graduate program. The dean further informed him that he would be eligible for a paid scholarship.

He worked part-time in the library which paid for part of his tuition and gave him a small amount of spending money, plus it allowed him to utilize the library's computers. In addition his father provided a monthly stipend. Not that he needed that much money as he led a rather ascetic lifestyle. A grant for graduate work would allow him to get a rental residence off-campus and perhaps an older used automobile. His only hobbies included going for hikes in the mountains, watching the hot-air balloons, and of course surfing the web.

In September 2001, he moved off-campus and began graduate studies. However, the events of September 11, 2001 had a devastating impact on him. After the attacks of the Twin Towers and the pentagon, Yousef's life was forever changed. His American classmates took to calling him "Joe the Taliban." He became even more withdrawn and attended the local mosque with a religious fervor.

At the mosque, he met other disenchanted Islamic students. As a graduate student, he became their surrogate *Leader*. Known for his judicious wisdom and thoughtful approach, Yousef was admired by the other Muslim students and often led religious discussions at the mosque.

Even though the foreign Muslim students were in the United States voluntarily, after the events following 9/11, they all experienced some anti-Muslim sentiment in their dealings with their American classmates. Yousef took on the role of mentor, counselor, and leader.

The introspective Yousef, sighed to himself "this is my destiny!" "Insha'Allah," he repeated to himself.

CHAPTER 3

ANTHONY GARZA WAS the FBI Special Agent assigned as a liaison with the New Mexico Department of Homeland Security and Emergency Management, better known as the "fusion center." Although, Garza worked out of the Albuquerque FBI field office, he made a trip to the Santa Fe fusion center on a regular basis.

SA Garza was known as a hard charging detective with a quick wit, and an impulsive approach to crime solving. Divorced once, he was sometimes known as a "ladies man" because of his masculine appearance. Garza had a heavy well-defined chin, distinct nose, and thick curly black hair. He also took care of his body with daily workouts in the gym, and long early morning jogs in the dry, high altitude of Northwest Albuquerque.

On this third week of August, SA Garza was on his way to Santa Fe via interstate 25 to visit the N.M. fusion center. He was immediately struck by the thick smell of smoke along with the accompanying gray haze on the horizon. Arriving just after 10:00 in the morning, he planned his weekly meeting with Sharon Martinez. Sharon was an intelligence analyst with the fusion center.

Sharon was very attractive, and single. Although, she was ten years younger than the 40 year old Garza, both Sharon and

Tony (as she called him) seem to hit it off together. Although, no actual romance had occurred, Sharon was eager that something might happen in near future. She also realized that Tony was the consummate professional, never willing to cross the line between professional ethics and personal inclinations. Sharon supposed because of Tony's strong moral compass coupled with his masculine character is why she was reflexively drawn to him.

When Garza arrived Sharon was busy at her "secret" computer assessing the damage due to yesterday's wave of forest fires.

"Hi Shar," whispered Tony as he made his way to her cubicle.

"Hello Tony, I can't believe all the smoke in the air—it smells like an ashtray in here."

"You bet—we received a RFI from headquarters this A.M. HQ thinks it might have a terrorist nexus. You picking up any chatter?"

"Nothing definitive Tony, however I'm trying to pin down data on an extremist group in the Albuquerque university area. You hear anything?"

"Negative," Tony exclaimed, while nervously tapping the tips of his fingers on a nearby desk.

"It's almost lunch time Shar, why don't you escort me to another one of them superb Santa Fe eating establishments, and tomorrow I'll check out your radical group theory."

CHAPTER 4

Yousef Khan had sent off his protégés on their respective missions. Phase one of this endeavor was almost complete. Media reports had concluded that the great America was devastated, shocked, and confounded. He sat confidently at his humble residence and assessed updated news accounts from his computer. In his mind, the premise of *Occam's razor* came to mind, "the simplest way to do something is likely the best way." Sending out his group of devoted colleagues to strike the American infidels when and where they could not defend themselves had been a stroke of pure brilliance.

Yousef was about to enter phase two of his venture—an undertaking that only he, the great leader, who had the cleverness, thoughtful preparation, and the intellectual capacity to execute. "Insha'Allah."

He had purchased a 1994 Toyota Tacoma truck when he started graduate school. This vehicle allowed him to live off-campus and rent a small single family dwelling a short distance from the university. It also permitted him to venture into the nearby Sandia Mountains to hike and reflect. Furthermore, it allowed him to travel to Balloon Fiesta Park and watch the hot-air balloons dance with the clouds.

On one such adventure to Balloon Fiesta Park, a man asked Yousef if he would like to "go up" with him. Shy, reserved Khan nodded in the affirmative. He helped the man carefully lay out the deflated nylon fabric. Next the man turned on an enormous fan, partially engorging the balloon. Finally the man turned on the burner which was connected to a propane tank and delivered hot air into the throat of the balloon. The "envelope," as the man referred to the balloon, quickly expanded and gradually began to rise, righting the wicker basket or "gondola" as the man called it.

"Hop in," the man shouted, while he adjusted the burner— further expanding the balloon.

Yousef was instantly mesmerized. Floating among the clouds, soundless except for the burner constantly being adjusted, he was totally captivated. The man explained how the heated air controlled the balloon's elevation, and depending on altitude, the horizontal direction was dependent on catching the right wind stream. The man allowed Yousef to take control of the burner detailing the theory of hot-air balloon flight.

"You're a natural," remarked the man, as Yousef adjusted the instruments.

On various occasions throughout the ensuing months the man invited Yousef along to enjoy the sensation of hot-air ballooning. During one outing as their balloon was drifting along towards the southeast corridor of the city, the man advised Yousef to "pull up."

"We're heading toward Kirtland Air Force Base," said the man. "Several military installations have restrictions on violating their airspace. We need to pull up to change direction."

"What happens if we cannot control the balloon and we enter the restricted area?" asked Yousef.

"Nothing really," said the man. "Actually, last year I caught a sudden down draft and was forced to land in the middle of the base. When I landed I was met by a group of military security folks who helped me load up my balloon and gear. Then, I was escorted off base where I met up with my ground crew. I was really embarrassed, but the folks at the base were very polite and understanding."

Yousef nodded.

CHAPTER 5

SA GARZA HAD scheduled a meeting with the University of New Mexico's dean of students at 08:00, the following day, based on his discussions with Sharon.

At 07:50, he arrived at the dean's office and was greeted by his administrative assistant just outside the academic administrator's office. "Dean Tolson will be right with you Mr. Garza."

At precisely 08:00, Dean Tolson departed his office and extended his hand to SA Garza, while inviting him into his office.

Dean Tolson was a smallish man with a bad comb over and an "officious" nature. Garza showed Tolson his FBI credentials and further explained that he was acting on information concerning "radical groups" at the university. The ever bureaucratic Tolson seemed rather taken aback by Garza's statement. Garza preceded further and asked permission to chat with some of the professors at the university.

"Absolutely not!" shrieked Tolson, "Our students and this university have confidentiality matters to maintain."

"Even if concerns national security?" rejoined Garza.

"I won't have my students subject to unwarranted investigations," firmly stated the dean, "unless, of course you can provide me with some substantiated evidence of wrongdoing."

"Our investigation is not that far along," Garza advised.

"Then this meeting is over," clarified Tolson.

Garza let himself out of the dean's office and vacated the building. He located his government vehicle in the visitor parking lot, and drove back to his field office. Driving back to his office, Garza contemplated his next move. He decided he would check in with Sharon and determine if she could come up with any "actionable" intelligence based on her analysis.

Upon Garza's return to his office—he was informed of a "law enforcement sensitive" document that the field office had just received.

Law Enforcement Sensitive

The California Highway Patrol is holding in their San Bernardino County lockup facility two suspect males. The two men were observed in the Big Bear Lake area, acting suspicious and trespassing on private land. A neighboring resident observed their behavior and contacted local authorities. The California Highway Patrol was contacted. A local officer was in the vicinity and responded to the 911 call. He observed a 1992 Ford Taurus with New Mexico plates (#359 NWN) driving slowly along Highway 18 (Rim of the World Highway) in Big Bear Lake. Following the vehicle for approximately two miles where the officer watched the vehicle pull off of the highway and onto an unpaved surface road. As the officer approached the vehicle he noticed that there were two occupants in the vehicle. The officer observed that the passenger in the vehicle was leaning over into the rear seat and acting in an animated manner. The officer exited his automobile and approached subject vehicle on the drivers' side. The officer asked to see the driver's vehicle license and registration. Upon receipt the officer noted that the New Mexico license was issued to a Mr. Ali Jawed. The officer inquired as to what Mr. Jawed and his companion were doing in the area. Mr. Jawed replied the he and his friend were classmates and touring the area during summer break. When the officer asked what the two men were doing on this particular road, Mr. Jawed replied that they were lost and pulled off of the highway to look at a map. The officer then inquired as to what was under the blanket in the rear seat. Jawed replied, that it was nothing. The officer then requested if he could look for himself and Jawed responded in the affirmative. The officer opened the rear door on the driver's side and lifted a soiled blanket revealing a cardboard box containing twelve unused roadside safety flares. The officer inquired as to the use of flares, and the passenger replied that they were for safety reasons. The officer then requested ID for the passenger. The passenger stated that he was a student at the University of New Mexico and attending the school on an F-1 Student Visa. When the officer asked to see the visa, the passenger told him that he did not have it in his possession. The officer then suggested both men accompany him back to the station where they could resolve any issues. At this point the driver of the vehicle started his vehicle and attempted to flee the area. The officer initiated pursuit and called for backup. The subject vehicle was eventually stopped and the occupants arrested. Since arrest, both subjects refuse to answer any further questions. Subsequent examination of vehicle registration revealed impounded vehicle registered to a Mr. Ali Jawed (U.S. residence Albuquerque N.M.). Upon arrest and search of the passenger of said vehicle, said passenger possessed identification of a Mr. Mohammad Kazmi (also showing residence in Albuquerque N.M.).

Filed: Sgt. Frank Sturgent, CHP 768, 13:34, 08/23/02

CHAPTER 6

UPON READING THE document from California, SA Garza phoned one of his contacts at ICE, the U.S. Immigration and Customs Enforcement service. He requested status and residence information for Mohammad Kazmi and Ali Jawed. After looking into the federal data base, the federal agent informed Garza that both individuals were from Pakistan, both had legal student visas. Further, the two men were full time undergraduate students at the University of New Mexico where they resided on campus. Thanking the ICE agent, he then called the U.S. attorney's office in San Bernardino, California. He informed the chief prosecutor about the two individuals being held in the San Bernardino county lockup facility, and mentioned that because of a possible terrorist connection the FBI had the lead. Further, he advised the prosecutor that he was seeking a warrant to examine their dwelling and instructed the attorney to hold the two men until he got back in touch with him.

Next Garza filled out the documents required for a search warrant, and sent the office administrator to have a standing federal judge sign the warrant. Smiling to himself, he called Dean Tolson. Once he had him on the phone, Garza enlightened Tolson as to the newly determined change of events. He informed the Dean, that later this afternoon, he would have a signed warrant and wanted access to both Kazmi's and Jawed's rooms, but in addition, their class transcripts along with a list of current and former teachers at the university. Tolson paused over the telephone, started to object—paused again and finally relented. Next he called Sharon Martinez and told her what had transpired throughout the morning. He explained that he was in the process of securing a warrant to search both men's dormitory rooms later in the afternoon.

"Tony, I want to go with you!"

Since Sharon was not a law enforcement official it was rather unorthodox for her to make this request. In addition, "intelligence analysts" typically sat behind their desks and did not do field work.

"I guess you deserve this one Shar, meet me at my office at 2:00 and we'll make the road trip together."

Chapter 7

In early summer Yousef Khan took lessons in order to become a "certified" hot-air balloon pilot, in accordance with FAA regulations. This action was required in order for him to legally rent an aircraft from an authorized leasing dealer. Mid August 2002, he rented such a craft in fulfillment of his mission. Most hot-air balloon pilots had a whole crew to support transport, ground assembly, and air operations. Yousef had perfected a system allowing him to perform all operations by himself. This permitted him to keep his mission clandestine, and be remembered as a true leader.

Once Yousef had dispatched his associates for phase one of the operation, he busily occupied himself achieving phase two, the most significant portion of his plan. This part of his plan was conceived and to be executed by him, and him alone.

He worked almost nonstop in his garage assembling his *Mother of Satan* bomb. He carefully scooped the powdered ammonium nitrate into the mouth of his iron pipe. Then he poured all the bottles of his procured nitro-methane fuel oil into a large plastic bucket. To the clear fuel oil he poured a small bottle of red food coloring and slowly mixed the liquid.

The food coloring additive allowed Yousef to verify that the fuel was adequately merged with the ammonium nitrate powder. He cautiously poured the liquid into the nitrate filled pipe. After this process was complete he used a dolly to transport the now filled pipe into his Toyota truck. The truck was already loaded with the hot-air balloon components to include a nylon envelope, 3-passenger basket, a double burner, and two 20 gallon propane tanks.

The last two items that he loaded into his truck were the cone-shaped end cap that he fabricated and the very sensitive powdered explosive he had produced. He gingerly took the explosive from his refrigerator and carefully placed the mixture into a Styrofoam container prior to putting it into the cab of his truck.

He formulated his plan when he was surfing the web and goggled "bomb." He was able to access a blog site that listed all locations for the entire U.S. nuclear stockpile. Further, he was able to "goggle map" specific locations with actual storage positions. He was amazed that he was actually able to view an overhead image of an actual storage location, with GPS coordinates. Yousef's brain spun, as he methodically devised his plan.

CHAPTER 8

SPECIAL AGENT GARZA met up with Sharon Martinez at his field office in Albuquerque at 13:26. He had obtained a search warrant and asked Sharon to jump into his government vehicle. His office was located in the Northwest of Albuquerque, while the university was situated in the Southeast, so the travel time would be close to forty-five minutes. The transit time would allow him time to think how he would proceed on this operation.

After arriving at the university, Tony walked with Sharon to the Administration Building. Once they entered the Dean of Students suite of offices, Tony mentioned to Sharon to let him do the talking.

When they entered the Dean's office, in addition to Tolson, two other men, and a woman were present. A nervous Tolson introduced, Adam Bradley—the Chief of Campus Police, Anna Gutteriez—a representative from the Registrars Office, and Dr. Ahmad—associate director of the Engineering Department.

After shaking hands, Garza introduced Sharon, "And this is Ms. Martinez, an official with the Department of Homeland Security."

A supercilious Tolson told Garza, "Mr. Bradley will accompany you to the two individuals' rooms. When you're finished there,

Miss Gutteriez will provide you with their academic records, along with the names of their teachers. Dr. Ahmad will then escort you to speak with any teachers, should you desire."

"We'll see," countered Garza. "Let's take this one step at a time." Garza and Martinez were then escorted by the campus Police Chief to examine the rooms.

Walking to student housing, the Chief informed Garza and Martinez, "Kazmi and Jawed are actually roommates sharing a two-bedroom dwelling, with a bath and small sitting room." Unlocking the door to the residence, the Chief began entering the confined space.

"Stay out here in the hallway," Garza said to the Chief. Pulling two pairs of latex gloves from his pocket, Garza handed one pair to Martinez. "Put these on, and do not touch anything," said Garza. The insouciant Martinez winked, nodded her head, and smiled broadly.

Garza stood suspended in the doorway examining the small space. A threadbare sofa occupied one wall, a tiny kitchen table along with two metal chairs rested against the opposite wall. Also nearby were a 19 inch Zenith television on a metal stand, a floor lamp, and a computer which took up most of the surface of the table. Garza walked into the cramped room and peered into one of the bedrooms. In the bedroom were a single bed frame and mattress, a small table and lamp, and a worn prayer rug. The bedroom had a small clothes closet with a few items of clothing laid out on shelves or hung neatly on a cross beam. The next bedroom was identical, with similar furnishings. As Garza backed-out from the second bedroom he discovered Sharon sitting at one of the metal chairs with the computer booted up.

"Sharon I thought I told you not to touch anything," roared Garza.

"Tony, look what I have already found!"

Garza peered over her shoulder and observed what she was looking at.

Sharon had pulled up Internet Explorer and accessed the "history" view.

"Just look Tony, starting with last week's web history; you can see what these guys have been looking at!" She scrolled down a list that appeared on the monitor:

Gama'a al-Islamiyya

HAMAS

Harakat

Ul-Mujahidin

Hizballah

Islamic Jihad Group

Jemaah Islamiya

Palestinian Islamic Jihad

Al-Qaida in the Islamic Maghreb

"So what Sharon, why wouldn't a Pakistani want to view Middle-Eastern websites?"

"These are not just any websites Tony, these are known terrorist websites."

Garza thought for a moment before replying, "Well I can't prosecute an individual based on what websites they visit."

Sharon somewhat flustered answered, "Tony, go busy yourself with something else—let me handle the computer."

Garza shook his head while initiating a detailed examination of the rest of the area.

Next Sharon clicked on the Microsoft Outlook icon. Soon she was reading emails sent to and from the computer.

Nearly an hour had elapsed and Garza clearly flustered, muttered, "Damn it, I can't find squat!"

An elated Sharon countered, "Just hold on, Tony. I'm starting to put this together."

Tony sat down next to Sharon and studied what she was working on. She had a piece of bond paper in front of her and as she read various emails, she made quick annotations to the paper. Soon she turned to Tony and exclaimed, "I think I've got it!"

Sharon informed Tony of her analysis. "Tony I went back several weeks reviewing all emails received and sent with this computer. At least 90% of the emails are communications from the same ten or eleven individuals. By their surnames, all appear to of Middle-Eastern decent. A few of the emails refer to *a mission, divine mission, or the mission.* Next, in the context of the mission, a timeline is alluded to as two days ago. This fits when the fires were first reported. In other emails, it references *the divine one, the little leader, or leader.* In another email it mentions *leader,* but indicates the name Yousef." Sharon had written down eleven names, some full names and some partial.

Tony hurried Sharon out of room and instructed the Campus Police Chief to seal off the room. He mentioned to the Chief that he would have a FBI forensics team arrive later that afternoon.

He then used his government Blackberry to telephone Dean Tolson and inform him that he was on his way back to the Dean's office and to have the representative from the Registrars Office, along with the rep from the Engineering Department in attendance when he arrived.

As they were walking to the dean's office, Garza mentioned to Sharon that they were now going to cross-reference the names that Sharon had written down against a data base of students attending the university. When they arrived at the Dean's office Tony showed Dean Tolson along with Anna Gutteriez from the Registrars Office, and Dr. Ahmad from the engineering department, the list that Sharon had compiled.

Of the eleven names, six were complete names with a first and last name, four names seemed to be last names, and one— "Yousef" could be either a first name or last name. Dean Tolson asked his secretary to make copies of the list for everyone. Upon inspection, Dr. Ahmad appeared visibly shaken. Garza discerning this behavior asked, "Dr. Ahmad what's the problem?"

"Some if not all of these names are students in my department," replied the stunned professor.

The six full names Dr. Ahmad confirmed were matriculated students, the four surnames the doctor could not positively identify, and Yousef he suggested was a common Pakistani spelling of the first name Joseph. Garza then asked if he had any students going by that first name. Dr. Kahn mentioned that he had a graduate student that was named Yousef, and that his last name was Khan.

Garza solicited more information on Yousef Khan. "Doctor, what can you tell me about Yousef Khan."

"Yousef Khan is not the type of person you are looking for. Little Joe is a fine student who is refined and respectful. He would never be involved with something illegal or to bring disrespect to his family."

"Please explain your "little Joe" reference, Doctor," inquired Sharon.

"Yousef Khan is a small gentleman, a number of the staff and students affectionately refer to him as *little Joe*, Joe being the anglicized Yousef," clarified Ahmad.

Garza instantly caught up with the path which Sharon was heading. "We need to see him right now!"

The woman from the Registrars Office called her office to obtain Yousef's room number and to find out if he had a phone number listed. Hanging up the phone, she reported, "Yousef Khan resides off campus with no telephone number listed."

"Give me the address," pleaded Gaza.

CHAPTER 9

INHALING THE PUNGENT odor from the smoldering landscape, Yousef Khan embarked on his final quest. Leaving his Albuquerque home just before noon, he gave himself plenty of time to reach his final destination. He had inventoried his cargo which he painstakingly packed into his vehicle.

He traveled along Interstate 40, ever mindful of observing all traffic regulations. By 8:45 that evening, Khan had reached his destination, the infamous "city of sin," Las Vegas. Las Vegas was the infidel's wicked city renowned for its wanton excesses and hedonistic overindulgence. The destruction of this evil city will serve as benchmark for all infidels that Allah's teachings shall be revered, Yousef thought. He also fanaticized about his place in history for taking part in such a glorious event.

Once Yousef arrived in Las Vegas he consulted his GPS instrument for directions to his eventual target. He merged onto Interstate 15 driving north for approximately fifteen minutes, before taking the Speedway boulevard exit. Five minutes later, he found himself at the entrance to Nellis Air Force Base. He was careful not attract any undue attention as he circled the perimeter of the base while checking with his GPS. Finally he arrived in a valley on the outskirts of base where he could visually identify his objective. He then searched for a region in the area where he could conceal himself prior to the execution of his plan.

Before sunrise the next morning Yousef rose from a night of erratic sleep in the cab of his truck. He hunted for a secure locale, upwind of the weapons storage area. He formulated his plan with scrupulous detail. His preparation included setting up his hot-air balloon in the cover of darkness before first light. When he at last found a secluded location in a mountainous field adjacent to the airbase, he checked his wind meter to determine the ideal airstream conditions. Finally, fidgety with excitement, Yousef begin to assemble his aircraft. Checking and double checking each stage of assembly, he muscled the partially assembled bomb into the wicker gondola. When the bomb was in place, he verified the operation of the trapdoor that he had constructed in the bottom quadrant of the basket. Confirming its functioning, he set about putting together the components of his masterwork.

He delicately attached the sugary white explosive to the front of the bomb. This would act as the "trigger" or initiator, as well as providing the "booster" to initiate the main nitrate explosive charge.

Ten minutes before daylight, he turned on the propane fueled burner. "Insha'Allah," recited Yousef.

CHAPTER 10

SA GARZA AND Sharon Martinez arrived at Yousef Khan's dwelling twenty minutes after leaving Dean Tolson's office. The home was located less than two miles from the university in Southeastern Albuquerque. The 1950s vintage abode was a Spanish styled home, with a red tile roof and a dirty off-white stucco exterior. The pea-gravel landscape had little in the way of plants or other ornamental decor. Performing a quick recon, Garza noticed a one car garage, a smallish backyard, and front and back doors with wrought-iron casings.

Garza asked Sharon to stay in the driveway while he ambled up to the front door. Knocking hard on wooden façade produced no results. He strolled to the rear of the house and banged on the entry with the same results. Almost giving up, he observed the rear door shift slightly with his last thump. Fingering the doorknob, he push gently and the door swung open. "Hello, anyone here," Garza shouted, as he entered what appeared to be the kitchen. Garza continued through the kitchen, passed a portico into what appeared to a combination living room— dining room area. He proceeded into another doorway which led into a single bedroom with a master bath at the far end.

The house was sparsely furnished and extremely small. Furnishings were flea-market castoffs. The only unusual item was a Middle-Eastern prayer rug, facing east, in the single bedroom. Exiting the rear of the home, Garza wanted to inspect the garage to see if a vehicle was present.

Sharon met Garza in the back yard as he muttered, "Nobody home."

SA Garza paced five steps to the side of garage, pushing open a wooden plank door. As the door opened, he was hit with an overpowering, acrid stench. He motioned Sharon back, as he made a hasty retreat out of the structure. Garza's eyes were watering excessively, and the stink overwhelmed his sinuses. "What is it, what is it?" screeched, Sharon.

"I think we've stumbled on a 'meth lab,'" Garza wheezed.

After a few moments Garza made a call to the Albuquerque Police Department. Identifying himself as Special Agent Garza with the FBI, Garza detailed the suspicious items that he encountered during his investigation. He gave the dispatcher the address and mentioned he would wait for the APD arrival. Next he called his FBI office and informed his supervisor of the day's events. He asked his supervisor to send a forensics team to the university, bag any items of interest—to include the computer, and to seal off all suspect rooms. He communicated to his boss, all the points of contact he had acquired at the university during his afternoon visit.

Twenty minutes later a phalanx of APD arrived including five patrol cars, a bomb disposal unit, a swat team, and a dog detection unit. The bomb disposal unit was dispatched because a "meth lab" is considered not only highly toxic, but posed a volatility hazard as well. Garza flashed his credentials and led the unit to the garage. The team was already dressed out in protective clothing with respirators. Peering into the building, the team chief paused to assemble in his mind what he was scrutinizing. He was very deliberate in his actions as he would step—stop—

examine, before making his way throughout the structure. His partner waiting near the entrance was called over by the team chief, and a dialog took place. All that Garza could observe was an animated pointing, along with a garbled communication under the respirators. Finally both men vacated the structure as they pulled off their respirators.

The team chief went up to Garza and declared, "That is not a meth lab in there. What are in there are the precursors for making explosives."

Garza's sole response was a hollow "shit."

CHAPTER 11

YOUSEF KHAN ASCENDED with his hot-air balloon through the dry, mountain air at sunrise. Gaining altitude, he tried to balance his aim of reaching a height that would allow the plummeting bomb to obtain terminal velocity but close enough to visually sight-in his target.

Multi-tasking to the max, he was able to study both the altimeter and wind speed indicators, while constantly adjusting the propane-fed burner. Focusing on the GPS, he navigated in a measured approach toward his intended mark. Sighting in on the middle portion of the vast field, Yousef selected the centermost section of the nuclear housed structures. Choosing the precise mark more or less at random, he turned up the burner to increase elevation. As he drifted over the target structure, he released the trapdoor mechanism releasing the bomb. "*Allah Akbar* (God is great)," Yousef screamed, as the missile glided into the structure.

As the projectile penetrated the earthen covered igloo, a colossal explosion ensued. This was followed by an enormous fire-ball erupting from the now vacant, crown of the edifice. Debris, smoke, and conflagration filled the atmosphere.

The initial detonation created a massive blast wave driving the balloon high into the air. Yousef was momentarily stunned by the searing heat and the powerful pressure. Temporarily elated that the bomb exploded as intended, he then wondered why he had survived the nuclear detonation. Then he began to comprehend, the nuclear weapons did not explode.

CHAPTER 12

SPECIAL AGENT GARZA contemplated his next move while dining with Sharon Martinez after an incredibly hectic day. Early reports from the forensics teams dispatched to the university suggested criminal involvement of at least ten Pakistani nationals not including one Yousef Khan. However, except for the two suspects being detained in California, the whereabouts of Khan and the remaining eight Pakistani's remained a mystery. APD put out a BOLO (be-on-the-look-out) bulletin with pictures from the UNM ID office, along with vehicle and drivers license information.

After ordering from a menu at a local New Mexican restaurant on the west side of Albuquerque, Garza decided, "I need to interview those two suspects being held in California."

Sharon agreed proposing, "Tony, I need to go with you."

"Sharon, this is really FBI business."

Not deterred, Sharon submitted, "Haven't I helped so far?"

"Ya Shar, but it might get a bit dicey knowing we are now chasing down real terrorists."

"That hasn't stopped me so far Tony," pleaded Sharon. "I'm calling my boss back in Santa Fe to get his permission, if he agrees I'm going with you!" Getting out of her seat, Sharon excused herself, heading to the women's room. Once out of earshot, Sharon pulled her cell phone from her purse and dialed her immediate supervisor's number. After he answered, Sharon relayed the events that emerged throughout the day. She then stated that she was planning to accompany the FBI the following day to interview the suspected terrorists in California. Sharon's supervisor did not respond, so Sharon added, "this is really a great opportunity for the Department of Homeland Security and especially our office."

After asking a few questions on the logistics of the trip, the supervisor concurred. Sharon promised to keep him posted with daily updates and hung-up her phone. With an effusive smile on her face Sharon returned to her seat in the restaurant.

"Well?" Tony inquired.

"My boss is all for it," countered Sharon. "He mentioned that it showed good interagency cooperation, the Department of Homeland Security and the Federal Bureau of Investigation, both partners taking on the 'War on Terrorism.'"

Their dinners arrived as Sharon took her seat. Tony had ordered a Carne Adovada Burrito with red and green chili, while Sharon selected Blue Corn Chicken Enchiladas smothered with cheese. As Sharon was biting into her entre, Tony suggested, "We better decide how we're traveling tomorrow."

Sharon offered, "I'll get a hotel room in Albuquerque tonight, and then meet you at the airport first thing in the morning."

"Sharon, that's dumb," Tony submitted, "Just stay at my place tonight, I've got two bedrooms and plenty of space."

"Okay," Sharon responded with a grin.

Finishing up their plates, the waitress returned with a large platter of sopapillas. Snatching one and pouring honey into one end, Tony declared, "These things are going to be the death of me!"

"I love them too!" Sharon acknowledged.

Tony drove Sharon to his FBI office to retrieve her automobile. After arrival, Tony whispered into her ear, "Just follow me, I just live ten minutes from here."

Minutes later, Tony pulled into the parking lot of a new, richly appointed, townhouse complex. After parking, Tony went over to Sharon's car, opened her door and escorted her to his front entrance. Once inside, Tony offered, "Make yourself at home, I've got some phone calls to make."

Sharon walked leisurely around Tony's home, taking in the furnishings. The dwelling was handsomely decorated with a mix of contemporary styling with a Tuscan influence. Antique oriental carpets adorned the wooden floors, and the furniture, while not heavy or overstated maintained a certain a Spanish elegance. Sharon also noted that the home was almost excessively clean and orderly.

Tony returned from a back bedroom and announced, "We're leaving on a Southwest flight at 7:45 in the morning, making a one hour stopover in Phoenix, and arriving at Ontario airport before noon. I've contacted the San Bernardino County DA and told them that we would like to interview the two suspects sometime in the early afternoon."

"Now Shar, let me show you your accommodations for tonight, then I'll treat you to one of my super margaritas, then we can turn-in for a big day tomorrow."

As they finished their drinks a large white cat jumped up onto the arm of the chair where Tony was sitting. Tony calmly scratched the feline and said, "this is peeve, my wandering kitty."

"Peeve?" asked Sharon.

"Yep. Peeve as in 'my pet peeve.'" Tony laughed.

"You're nuts!"

"Well we better turn-in; we have a long day tomorrow."

Rising early, Tony was shaved, showered, and dressed before Sharon entered from the spare bedroom. Making her way toward the main bathroom, Sharon announced, "Morning Tony, I'll be ready in fifteen minutes."

Tony was seated at the kitchen table busily fingering a laptop computer. "Take your time, its not even sunrise yet."

Thirty minutes later, Tony at the wheel of his government vehicle and Sharon in the passenger seat, were ten minutes away from the Albuquerque Sunport airport.

Tony's mind wandered throughout the drive. First and foremost he tried to anticipate what would await them upon their arrival in California but a secondary thought kept emerging, Sharon smelt good. She smelled clean, of soap or shampoo or something. He thought of complimenting her, but ever aware of his professional appearance he did not want to appear forward.

Sharon took casual glances at Tony during the drive. He appeared to be deep in thought and perhaps planning the day's agenda. Sharon wanted to engage Tony in conversation, but didn't want to distract Tony from his contemplation.

Tony dropped Sharon off at the ticketing entrance, while he deposited his car in the long-term parking lot. Sharon was speaking to a Southwest Airlines ticketing agent as Tony approached from the rear. "Here let's use my government credit card, and we'll sort out the details later," mumbled Tony.

There was a small queue of travelers waiting at the security checkpoint. Once they were processed and found their boarding gate, Sharon noticed a large group of people surrounding a television monitor viewing Sky news. Sharon pointed to the gaggle, and they both ambled in the direction of the crowd.

"What's going on?" Tony inquired to an onlooker.

"It appears a bomb just went off in Las Vegas," answered the bystander.

Chapter 13

Yousef Khan sat stunned, on the dry desert floor. The massive explosion which he created caused his hot-air balloon to veer out of control, and slammed into a mountain range. He was fortunate to escape relatively unharmed. He sat somewhat bewildered peering at the devastation in the valley below. Staggering to his feet, Yousef sorted out his options.

At last he decided that he must return to join his associates and once again act as their leader and mentor. His original plan was to sacrifice his own life while demonstrating to the American infidels that they could be conquered. In addition, he wanted to symbolize his death to his colleagues as the ultimate display of courage. "Insha'Allah," Yousef sighed.

Yousef decided that he could not return to his vehicle, as the infidels were already responding to the destruction below. He trekked along the steep rocky paths attempting to egress on the far side of the mountain range.

Wandering along the mountain range for several hours he came upon a trail that led him over several large hills. Eventually, he sighted a road to make his travel less arduous. He followed the road south which he hoped would take him back to Las Vegas. He assumed if he could get to the large city undetected, he would be lost in the crowd. Two hours passed, and Yousef could make out the Las Vegas skyline.

In early evening, Yousef had finally arrived in the heart of the city. Emergency vehicles with loudspeakers were traveling along the roadways insisting that everyone remain inside. He hid in the middle of a crowd of agitated strangers, and walked into an extravagant hotel. Once entering the hotel he looked for the men's restroom. When he located the restroom, he stood at the sink to cleanse his body. Glimpsing his face in a mirror, Yousef realized he had several small abrasions on the left side of his face. He did his best to wash these areas thoroughly and rinse the accumulated dust and sand from the rest of his body.

Chapter 14

Seven minutes after the "explosion" in the weapons storage area at Nellis Air Force Base, the base Command Post put calls out for members of Explosive Ordnance Disposal unit assigned to the 99th Civil Engineer Squadron to respond. Since the majority of the unit had not made their way into work that early in the morning, the Command Post exercised its recall roster. Forty-five minutes later, the first team, dressed out in protective clothing arrived approximately 3,000 meters outside, and upwind, of the detonation. Pulling out radiation detection instruments, and taking initial measurements, the team chief, Air Force Master Sergeant Tommy Dyer announced into his mouthpiece, "we're hot!" Taking, and recording measurements every twenty meters, the process was tedious and time-consuming.

Two-hours later, acting on the advice of the base hospital's health physicist, the Wing Commander decided to evacuate the base of all non-essential personnel.

Meanwhile, the Marine Corps Chemical Biological Incident Response Force, better known as CBIF was notified of the incident by U.S. Northern Command and had boots on the ground before noon. The Department of Energy's Federal Radiological Monitoring and Assessment Center, along with

Radiological Assistance Program, and the Nuclear Emergency Support Team were all in route to Las Vegas within two hours after being notified. Additionally, DOE's Aerial Measuring System aircraft was in the air three hours after notification taking radiological measurements to determine contamination levels to the Las Vegas area along with greater Clark County.

The Federal Emergency Management Agency (FEMA, Region 9), had notified the Las Vegas Fire Rescue Services to issue a public service warning for all residents to take shelter.

The local FBI Hazardous Materials Response Team was collecting samples outside the base perimeter ninety minutes after the explosion and came across the damaged hot-air balloon. The Las Vegas FBI field office had tracked the downed craft, back through the leasing agent in Albuquerque, New Mexico. Special Agents from the Albuquerque office had interviewed the rental manager later in the day, and determined that the balloon in question was rented twelve days earlier to a Mr. Yousef Khan.

CHAPTER 15

SA GARZA AND Sharon Martinez had to change planes in Phoenix to get to their final destination in California. While waiting to board their flight to Ontario, Garza busied himself talking on his cell and receiving updates from his Albuquerque office. Sharon was glued to the television monitor at their departure gate taking in the incredible events occurring in Las Vegas.

Finally boarding their flight, Sharon asked Tony if he thought the incident in Las Vegas had any connection to the fire setting terrorists that they were investigating. "I haven't thought about it Shar," remarked Tony. "Do you think there is a link?"

"I honestly don't know Tony. I just feel that it seems to be a rather remarkable coincidence," countered Sharon.

After arrival at the Ontario International Airport, Garza rented a car and a short time later they were traveling along interstate 10, heading east toward San Bernardino. Less than thirty minutes later, they were pulling into the San Bernardino County lockup facility.

When the two entered the building, Tony presented his FBI credentials. The county sheriff guard remarked, "We've been expecting you Agent Garza." The guard led Tony and Sharon to the rear of the complex. As they approached a grey painted metal door, the guard asked, "How do you want to do this, Agent Garza?"

"I want to do one prisoner at a time," Tony answered.

"Okay, you folks stay put, and I'll take the first suspect into the interrogation room. I'll be back momentarily," the guard declared.

Minutes later the guard returned and guided Tony and Sharon to a white painted concrete block enclosure. Cut into the room was a 6 foot by 4 foot viewing window.

The detainee was seated in a metal chair in front of a large stainless steel table. He rubbed, clenched and unclenched his hands excessively. He stared nervously toward the floor, breathing heavily.

Peering through the window, the guard whispered, "This one is Mohammad Kazmi, according to the ID that we took from him."

"He looks like a little boy," observed Sharon.

"Well both of the prisoners have been pretty quiet, they haven't answered any questions, haven't asked for a lawyer, haven't asked for anything. But when we put a tray of food in their cells, we come back a few minutes later, all the food is consumed," volunteered the guard.

Tony and Sharon entered the small room assuming positions on the opposite side of the table.

"I'm Special Agent Anthony Gaza with the FBI, and this is (gesturing toward Sharon), Ms. Sharon Martinez, with the Department of Homeland Security."

Next Tony pulled a small card from his wallet and proceeded to read the prisoner his "Miranda Rights."

Tony and Sharon took seats facing the prisoner. "Is your name Mohammad Kazmi," Tony commanded. The prisoner sat silent, gazing at the wall behind Tony. "Listen son, we're here to obtain some information." The young man sat rigidly, trembling slightly. "Do you know Yousef Khan?" With the mention of Khan's name, the young prisoner's hands started to shake. "Do you want to see Yousef?" Garza posed. The prisoner nodded faintly. Again Tony pursued, "Do you want me to bring Yousef here!"

The young man finally nodded and with a wavering voice, replied, "Yes."

"Tell us first," countered Tony, "about the mission that Yousef sent you on."

The young prisoner responded, "Yousef is our leader." Several minutes passed, and Tony was unable to elicit any more information from the prisoner. Tony then exited the room, and found the guard observing from the window. Garza instructed the guard to take Kazmi back to his cell.

When Kazmi was out of earshot, Tony asked Sharon, "Do you want to try this?"

"You bet Tony, I'll give it a try."

Tony and Sharon were already seated when the guard bought in Ali Jawed.

Sharon opened the conversation by introducing herself and Tony.

Tony then read the prisoner his "rights."

As with the first prisoner, the second prisoner sat rigid and afraid.

"Ali," Sharon whispered, "We have your leader, Yousef. He has asked us to come speak with you. Yousef has told us that he sent you out to start fires, is this true?"

"Yes," the prisoner nodded.

"Why would he ask you to do such a thing," inquired Sharon.

"To avenge Islam against the infidels," the young man stated as if by rote.

"Who gave Yousef his mission Ali?" Sharon asked.

"Yousef is our leader; his mission is decided by him."

"Tell us about Yousef's mission," queried Sharon.

"Yousef's mission is known only to Yousef."

After a few more minutes, Sharon gestured to Tony that she was ready to terminate the interview. Tony sought out the guard to return the prisoner to his cell.

Tony seemed deep in thought as he walked with Sharon back to his rental vehicle. "I'm wondering if Yousef deliberately kept members of his group in the dark," Tony suggested.

"Please explain," asked Sharon.

"Well," said Tony, "an effectively run covert group of terrorists is often times very compartmentalized. Compartmentalization allows the group or least the hierarchy to continue with their goals or operation when one of the bad guys is caught. In this case the group of bad guys that Yousef or whoever recruited, were recruited for one specific purpose. In this case, to start fires to disrupt and terrorize the American environment. They might have been left in the dark concerning the rest of the operations."

"Why would someone join such group? The wanton destruction of property that causes nothing but hate and disorder, it doesn't seem to help their cause, whatever their cause is."

"I guess we could speculate what motivates a terrorist. Religious fanaticism, a personal campaign against someone bigger than yourself, misguided ideals, or a crazy deluded mindset that violence against an oppressor, either real or imagined somehow settles a score."

"What score is that Tony?"

"I wish I knew Sharon, I wish I knew."

CHAPTER 16

AT 17:00 HOURS the Chairman of the Joints Chief of Staff had a previously unscheduled meeting in the Pentagon's secure briefing room known as "the Tank." Air Force Major General Bradley Thompson, Director of Nuclear Operations led the brief.

"At approximately 08:27 EST this A.M., a terrorist missile penetrated a nuclear weapons storage structure at Nellis AFB. Inside this particular structure were housed thirteen B53 high-yield thermonuclear bombs. These weapons are retired from active inventory. Once the missile pierced the earthen and concrete roof of the igloo, it was designed to detonate. Upon detonation the missile threw heated, steel fragments, piercing the alloy case of stored B53s inside the igloo, and ultimately leading to the detonation of the conventional (not IHE) high explosives inside the bombs. Due to the design features of the B53, no nuclear reaction occurred.

Within an hour base EOD responded to the incident, and determined radioactive contamination present throughout the weapons storage area and extending outwards beyond the perimeter of the base. Upon consultation with health professionals and recognized experts at the National Nuclear Security Administration, the Wing Commander evacuated all non-essential personnel. This included prisoners being held at the minimum security prison located less than one mile from the weapons storage area (audible laughs heard in the background).

First responders arrived at the scene to further assess contamination. These include, but are not limited to the following: DOE/NNSA, the Marine Corps Incident Response Force, Corps of Engineers—Rapid Response units, and various military Civil Support units. Additionally several other federal agencies are in route. These include FEMA, EPA, and other state, local, and tribal emergency responders.

The FBI is the lead law enforcement agency and the Nellis Air Force Base Wing Commander has set up an Incident Command System for the FBI on base proper.

At present, no casualties have occurred related to this incident, and initial reports from NNSA have suggested very low dosages for the city of Las Vegas, and the surrounding areas of Clark County. The Corps of Engineers has promised a detailed decon plan within a day or two.

Sir, working with our Air Force security folks, we have performed an initial vulnerability assessment of all our storage areas. With the exception of the underground facility at Kirtland, all of our weapons storage areas are aboveground. These sites are located at (pointing to a map displayed on a screen) Warren, Malmstrom, Minot, Barksdale, Whiteman, and of course Nellis. And of course the Navy has storage sites at Bangor and Kings Bay. This list is CONUS only, and does not include our OCONUS storage locations.

The security assessment indicates that all above ground storage sites are vulnerable to a vertical or overhead threat.

Further, we have asked the Civil Engineers at AFCESA to give us a ROM (rough order of magnitude) as to the cost and scope of burying our weapons. Using Kirtland as a model, their initial estimates are in the tens of billons of dollars and several years to complete.

Sir, subject to your questions, this completes my brief."

"Yeah Brad, I've got a few for you," responded General Caudwell.

"First off, why in the hell are we still storing obsolete weapons?"

"Sir, my understanding is that it is a 'through-put' issue at the Pantex Plant in Texas. They only have the facilities to dismantle so many weapons at any given time."

"Remind me to setup a meet with NNSA sometime in the future," rejoined Caudwell.

"Next question Brad, were all of the explosives consumed in the blast?"

"Sir, we believe so. As I mentioned earlier the conventional explosive used in the B-53 is not insensitive to shock and heat. The actual explosive, 'cyclotol' is a combination of RDX and TNT. From an overhead, aerial image the Commander sent us, all we could see was a smoking hole. Of course the fissile material, highly enriched uranium, was scattered during the detonation. The Wing Commander also told us that, incident to the detonation; there were numerous small fires throughout the storage area. We do not specifically know if these were caused by 'hot frag' landing in the brush, or 'kick- outs' of burning explosive."

"Okay, thanks Brad," responded General Caudwell. "I'm meeting the President in just over an hour at the White House, are there any final questions, anybody?"

"Sir, yes sir, I have one. I'm Major Joe Cattel from A3." Officers below the rank of O-6 do not traditionally have a speaking part in "the Tank," normally, they're brought along as scribes or note takers.

"Sir, why don't we just get rid of them?' suggested the Major.

"Get rid of what, Major?" countered the General.

"Sir, get rid of the whole nuclear stockpile," Cattel went on to explain. "Using the U.S. nuclear arsenal as a 'deterrent' no longer makes since. The cold war is over and the major nuclear nation-states like Russia and China would never think of going nuclear with us, especially when we could take them out with our advanced technology and superior conventional forces. The same could be said for the third world nations like North Korea, and Iran. We can surgically strike at will. Plus, how can the U.S. demand that North Korea, and Iran, not develop a nuclear capability, when we ourselves have the capability. Besides, do you think having a nuclear weapon is a deterrent to a terrorist? A terrorist does not care. A terrorist just uses our nuclear arsenal against us."

"Are you finished Major?" rejoined Caudwell.

"Sir, no sir, one last point. The United States could take the 'moral' high ground. By completely dismantling our entire nuclear stockpile, we the U.S., can lead by example. In showing developing countries that nuclear weapons are bad, we illustrate by getting rid of ours. This encourages all countries to disarm; again we 'lead by example.' Plus the added benefit, the money saved by disarming, could be applied to our already superior technology, further enhancing our position. I'm finished sir."

The General smirked slightly, "thank you Major."

Rising, General Caudwell announced, "Okay folks—I've got to go."

Walking behind General Caudwell, Lieutenant General Sutton, the A2, quipped to Major General Bradley Thompson, "Brad, can't you keep a muzzle on your Major?"

General Caudwell overheard the remark, turned and addressed the Air Force officers, "If you can't utilize Major Cattel's obvious talents, then I'm certain, I can find a position for him on the Joint Staff."

Lieutenant General Sutton paled, and nervously walked away.

General Caudwell pondered the Major's remarks as he walked back to his office. Taking the "moral high ground" and "leading by example" were phrases that resonated into his mind. Additionally, he contemplated the tremendous cost of protecting our strategic nuclear arsenal along with the associated vulnerabilities. Finally the General reflected on the global events shaping the world since 9/11.

"Our planet has changed," the General mused to himself, "and perhaps our defense posture should evolve as well." Deep in thought, he hurried back to his office.

CHAPTER 17

GENERAL LAWRENCE CAUDWELL had meeting at the White House to brief the president at 18:00 hours. When he arrived at the Oval Office, he was joined by David Pichman, Secretary of the Department of Homeland Security, William Tigger, FBI Director, and James Goodsell, National Security Advisor.

When the President arrived the FBI Director provided him with a short update. "Mr. President, all we have at this time, is that we believe that the fires in the Southwest states and this mornings bombing at Nellis Air Force Base are linked to a small, independent Muslim radical cell located in New Mexico. We have apprehended two alleged suspects and they are currently being held in a county lockup facility in southern California. We believe that this 'lone wolf' group has at least nine other members based on information we downloaded from the suspects personal computers. We have a BOLO sent to all law enforcement agencies at this time. That is all, Mr. President."

"Okay Bill, please keep me advised of any updates," requested the President.

"General, what can you tell me?"

General Caudwell referred to notes compiled earlier at the Pentagon. He gave the POTUS a succinct breakdown of the current assessment. "Sir, I would like to mention that to take care of this potential vulnerability in future, it might be advisable to retire the entire nuclear strategic stockpile." The General went on to highlight the statements uttered by the young Air Force Major just an hour earlier. "Sir he made a lot of sense, 'Take the moral high ground', and 'lead by example,' especially stuck in my craw."

After a short discussion, the President dismissed his advisors and sat down at his desk to pen notes for his speech to be delivered at 8 PM ET.

CHAPTER 18

"MY FELLOW AMERICANS, during the last 72 hours our way of life, and our freedoms came under attack in a series of deliberate and cowardly terrorist acts. Three days ago a succession of uncontrolled fires in the Southwestern United States were realized. We have reason to believe these fires were calculated and planned acts of intimidation. More recently, early this morning, an Air Force facility in Nevada was intentionally bombed, intended to strike at America's national strategic nuclear stockpile.

America was targeted for attack because we're the brightest beacon for liberty and opportunity in the world. And no one will keep that light from shining. A great people have been moved to defend a great nation. Terrorist attacks can distress our safety as a nation; however it will never deter our united resolve.

I have implemented our government's emergency response plans. Our military is powerful, and it's prepared. Our emergency teams are working in Nevada to manage the damage, along with the brave fire fighters working to control the pointless devastation to our forests and homeland.

The search is underway for those behind these evil acts. I've directed the full resources of our intelligence and law enforcement communities to find those responsible and to bring them to justice.

We will make no distinction between terrorists who committed these horrendous acts and those who harbor them.

I would like to thank the many world leaders who have called to offer their condolences and assistance. Upon consultation with the Chairman of the Joint Chiefs, General Larry Caudwell, I have decided, effective immediately, **to retire our entire nuclear weapons stockpile.** *I challenge all nations-states to do the same.*

America and our allies join with all those who want peace and security in the world. By ridding ourselves of the nuclear arsenal, America demonstrates this commitment and determination. From this day forward each American will unite for peace and justice. We go forward to defend freedom and all that is good and just in our world."

Following the President's speech, media pundits lavished praise and others condemnation.

Retired U.S. General Mark Witmark, excoriated the President's remarks regarding the retirement of nuclear arsenal as; "simplistic, and uninformed."

The Union of Concerned Scientists issued the following statement: "This stunning reversal in U.S. nuclear policy heralds a new and visionary approach to the elimination of nuclear weapons."

Media bloggers and journalists erupted into a frenzied account of the President's remarks concerning the retirement of the U.S. nuclear arsenal. Security pundits abounded giving their viewpoints and counterpoints regarding the new U.S. nuclear policy. Foreign affairs correspondents interviewed world leaders with opinions that spanned the spectrum from "the American president is disingenuous," to "he (POTUS) should be awarded the Nobel Peace Prize."

CHAPTER 19

SPECIAL AGENT GARZA and Sharon Martinez took the last available flight back to Albuquerque. As they left the Albuquerque airport, Tony called into his office to get the latest update on Yousef Khan.

"Anything new Tony?" Sharon queried as they got into his SUV.

"Just what we already know, local Las Vegas authorities have verified the truck found just outside the detonation site, is in fact Khan's, whereabouts still unknown."

Driving North on I-25, Sharon asked Tony if he could take the Coors boulevard exit, "I'd like to make a quick stop at Cottonwood Mall, Tony. I really need to buy a few clothing items and some toiletries. Wearing the same clothes two days in a row makes me feel disgusting."

"You betchya," Tony complied.

Returning to Tony's townhouse, Sharon and Tony both decided to turn-in and get some well-deserved rest, ready to face another day in the morning.

The next morning Sharon woke at 7 A.M. When she walked into the kitchen area she found Tony already showered and dressed, sitting at the kitchen table, poring over a lined legal pad.

"Pour yourself some coffee Shar, I'm just ruminating here. Whenever I'm working a case I list all of the knowns and unknowns. This allows me to list another column which is my gut-check list. My gut-check list provides me with unproven assumptions, and how best to proceed."

"What is your visceral list telling you?" inquired Sharon.

"One, based on what we obtained from the other suspects, I do not believe they knew what Yousef Khan was planning. Two, based on what Khan did plan, I believe he planned to die in the explosion, to be remembered as a martyr. Three, since we have to assume that he did survive, my gut tells me he will return home to strike another day."

"Why would he return to Albuquerque, when he has to know that authorities would be on the lookout for him?"

"Because this is the only city he has known for the last three and a half years. Because he feels a certain connection here and because to complete his mission, he has to strike again."

"Where do we start?" asked Sharon

"I don't know," Tony muttered.

Tony sat mulling over his next action with Khan. His thoughts also included Sharon. While she was getting dressed in the spare bedroom, he deliberated about working with Sharon and decided that they were a great team. She brought a certain element of inquisitive perspective without seeming intrusive or questioning unlike some of his FBI partners in the past. Tony liked working with Sharon.

Chapter 20

A DISHEARTENED YOUSEF Khan wandered the lobby of the Venetian Resort Hotel. He saw grandeur at every turn with the intricate chandeliers, extensive overhead paintings, marble floors, elaborate sculptures, and elegant marble columns. He shook his head at the incredible display of Western excess. Dejected, he drifted upwards toward the "hospitality parlor."

In the largely vacant parlor, he took a seat at a richly covered sofa. He found himself facing a large television screen. Suddenly the image of the United States President appeared on the monitor. He seemed drawn to the president's image, and at the same time repulsed. He heard the president speak of terrorist acts and labeled the terrorists as cowards and evil. He balled his hands into fists and tried to keep the tears from leaking out of his eyes. Soon he had fallen asleep.

While in slumber, he had a dream. He dreamt that the "Prophet" had a vital mission for him to complete. The Prophet instructed him to prepare himself for his next assignment by sustaining his intellect and maintaining his courage. The Prophet directed him to return to Albuquerque and to look for signs.

Recalling his dream, he felt again reinvigorated. Although his bomb did not produce the nuclear devastation and ruin that he had intended, it did awaken the Western infidels. It showed them that they were largely powerless to control the seemingly weaker inhabitants of the world, armed with consummate cunning and bravery.

Yousef again returned to his sleep with a calm resolve that he would strike another day.

Before dawn, an astonished Yousef awoke with a startled forbearance. He hurried out of the hotel and located the Greyhound Bus station, which he had passed the day before. He purchased a ticket back home. "Insha'Allah," he chanted to himself.

Chapter 21

While Sharon Martinez finished getting dressed, SA Garza called into his FBI field office and was told that the Albuquerque police had apprehended six more of the alleged student terrorists. They were currently being held in a downtown Albuquerque detention facility.

As a fully clad Sharon entered the living area, Tony calmly murmured, "Let's get moving, they've caught six more of the Pakistanis."

Driving into downtown Albuquerque, Tony explained to Sharon that his FBI colleagues' along with the metro police had staked out the students rooms at the university. When they returned at varied time intervals, our guys just nabbed them. We still have law enforcement officials standing-by at the university to see who shows up next.

"They can't be that dumb," said Sharon. "They had to know we'd be checking out their rooms by now."

"Evidently not," whispered Tony.

When SA Garza and Sharon Martinez entered the detention facility, they were informed that federal agents were currently interrogating the prisoners. After thirty minutes, two men walked past where Tony and Sharon were impatiently waiting.

"Hey what's up Tony!" shouted one of the men.

"Hi Tom," replied Tony. "Have you met Sharon?"

"I have not had the pleasure," answered Tom.

Tony introduced Sharon to the two FBI Special Agents.

"Well what did ya get," asked Tony.

"Not a lot," replied Tom. "We were notified that the first two suspects were bought in about two o'clock this morning. Jon and I got here around three to interview the first two, and as we were finishing up, four more were bought in. We just finished up with them."

Focused on his notes, Tom went on to mention, "They're all are pretty mute. But we eventually learned that they do in fact know each other. Attend the same mosque, and some are in the same classes at UNM. We did confirm that their spiritual leader—advisor, whatever you want to call him, is Yousef Khan, as we got off of your report from yesterday. We also confirmed that there are eleven members in this little group, also in line with your report."

"Did they mention specifically what mosque that they attend?" inquired Tony.

"Ya, it's that one down on Central near the university."

"Where do want us to go now?" solicited Tom.

"Just stay in contact with APD, and the university, we'll see what happens," suggested Tony.

"Sharon and I have a date at the mosque. Let's go Shar."

Getting into their vehicle, Sharon asked Tony how he would proceed once they arrived at the mosque.

"Will see what develops. Keep your eye out for body language and non-verbal actions. Sometimes I think we reveal more by what we don't say as oppose to actual verbal responses."

"That's very telling Tony. So what would you like to tell me?"

"What do you mean Sharon?"

"Well for starters Tony, we've been in each others company for the last three days. And in those three days, I haven't learned much about you. You're rather quiet, a loner, and a real law enforcement pro. But other than that, I don't know what makes you happy or sad, where you came from, or what is going on in that mind of yours."

"I'm sorry Shar, I didn't realize I was being so mysterious. As an explanation, sometimes I'm rather socially aloof. Most of the time my mind is occupied or focused on the case. Okay?"

"Okay for now Tony—just loosen up a bit, okay? I won't bite—and I won't file a harassment suit against you for saying something I might take issue with. Just be yourself."

Arriving in Old Town Albuquerque, Tony smiled and mimicked, "okay."

CHAPTER 22

THE GREYHOUND BUS had a forty-five minute layover in Flagstaff, Arizona. An elderly Hispanic woman occupying a seat next to Yousef asked him a question in Spanish. Since he had shaved his wispy black beard and cut his flowing, unruly hair, the lady assumed that Yousef was a Hispanic of some flavor. "*No comprenda,*" he politely intoned. Because of his dark complexion, he could easily be mistaken for a Latino.

The bus parked in the parking lot of a large strip mall. "Be back by 2:45," hollered the driver.

Yousef departed the bus to stretch his legs. As he walked along the storefronts, he noticed a banner on a shop window advising, "*We sell remote controlled model airplanes.*" He entered the establishment and strolled down the aisles observing the many displays. "*Super fuel for your super replica!*" read one exhibit. Yousef focused on the product, "Nitro-methane," he murmured to himself. He purchased a two litter bottle and boarded the bus.

The elderly woman was already in her seat, eating delicately from a number of foil wrapped bundles. "*Por favor,*" the woman sighed, gesturing to her food.

"*Gracias!*" Yousef mumbled, as he shared the aged-woman's lunch.

After the devouring much of the food, he thanked the lady again, and reclined his seat and closed his eyes. Soon he was sound asleep. He slept dreaming of his next mission. His goal was to bring the American oppressor to knees, hitting them at a time and place of his choosing. His ultimate objective was to be revered by his Muslim brothers and be remembered for his brilliance and sacrifice.

Waking with a start almost three hours later, he smirked to himself and mouthed, "Insha'Allah."

CHAPTER 23

OLD TOWN IS the historic district in Albuquerque dating back to the founding of the city by the Spanish in 1706. Most of the structures are constructed from adobe, and are grouped around a central plaza. The early Spanish settlers were religious people, and the first building erected was the San Felipe de Neri Church which still stands today.

Just outside of the Old Town area in stark contrast to Albuquerque's catholic heritage, is the Askari Mosque. This converted old adobe, was first built to house a wealthy colonial landowner. The only resemblance to a traditional mosque is a hand-shaped minaret pointing skyward from the flat roof of the original structure. A number of shabby out-buildings surrounded the central adobe edifice.

As SA Garza and Sharon Martinez parked their car, they become aware of a number men clustered about the portal of what they believed to be the main entrance. The men were clad in loose fitting, shirt like robes, which almost reached their ankles. All the men had unkempt facial hair, and bare feet. Tony approached the group and received callous stares in return. Sharon maintained her distance, halfway between the car and the entrance to mosque.

Tony greeted the men, however received no acknowledgement. "I would like to speak to your religious leader!" Tony stated firmly. Again, getting only blank glances from the assembly, Tony moved closer.

A figure appeared in the doorway. Covered in the same garment as the group of men, but with a skullcap, an old man emerged from the entryway. He had an abundant grey beard, which, strangely enough, was dyed reddish-orange at the bottom. "I am Imam Saadi, how can I assist you."

"Sir, I would like to speak with the religious cleric or leader," responded Tony.

"I am the Imam for this mosque," replied the unctuous Saadi.

"How do I address you?" asked Tony.

"As Iman Saadi," droned Saadi.

"Imam Saadi, I'm Special Agent Garza with the FBI, and standing next to my vehicle is Sharon Martinez, with the Department of Homeland Security, we would like a private audience with you," Tony stated flatly.

"Special Agent Garza, the woman's arms are not covered. I'm so sorry, but I can not bring her in this Mosque," posited the disingenuous cleric.

"Imam, if I can get a garment to cover her arms, can we come in and discuss a private matter?" inquired Tony.

"I'll try my best to accommodate you," the Imam whined.

"We'll be back in 30 minutes," shouted Tony, as he escorted Sharon back to the car.

Chapter 24

Meditating on the thirteen hour journey back to Albuquerque, Yousef methodically formulated his plan.

"Allah will provide the signs," thought Khan.

Traveling East on interstate 40, he gazed out at the desert landscape and drifted in and out of a semi-fugue state. He felt that he was receiving messages directly from Allah. Although he was unable to discern specifics, he accepted his fate as it was designed to unfold. He took comfort in knowing that a higher being was watching over him. He thought of his arrival back in Albuquerque and tried to anticipate what awaited him. He considered his life since arriving in the American city, his studies and his difficulties with the American students. "They have treated me as a dull child, always with ridicule and contempt," he contemplated, "and I will avenge myself, my family, and my faith."

Finally, he reflected on his life growing up in Pakistan, he thought of his mother and father and younger brothers and sisters. He wanted to make his family proud of him. He vowed to himself that he would accomplish his next mission, and be remembered as a true savior.

The kind old lady sitting next to him had not spoken since their luncheon meal. The only communication she afforded was a slight smile or an abbreviated nod of her head. She must be a sign, Yousef concluded. He quickly fell back into a deep sleep.

CHAPTER 25

"I DEFINITELY DO not trust the Imam!" barked Sharon as they departed the mosque.

"Neither do I!" Tony offered.

"Let's go back to your office so I can get access to a classified computer. I need to do some research on Imam Saadi."

"But I just told him that we would return within 30 minutes," said Tony.

"Let him wait. The better prepared we are when we are 'finally' allowed to speak with him, will give us an edge." suggested Sharon.

"Besides after I determine what is out there on him, we can stop by your place and I can pick up a long sleeve shirt, to make the Imam happy."

Tony and Sharon made the forty-five minute drive to the FBI office. Arriving inside, Tony led Sharon to a secure computer allowing Sharon access to various classified databases. In the meantime, Tony phoned a friend at the Albuquerque office of Immigration and Customs Enforcement, better known as ICE.

Tony asked his ICE acquaintance what he could dig up on an Imam Saadi. After a few minutes his colleague was able to determine that the Imam Hasan Saadi was born in Palestine in

1954 to Hamid Saadi (father) and Malika Hamidi-Saadi (mother). He came to the United States via London, England, in 1994. He obtained a Permanent Residence Card (commonly called a green card) in Detroit, Michigan in November 1994. Saadi worked as a cleric in the Detroit area for five years. In December 1999, Saadi applied to the U.S. Citizenship and Immigration Services to become a naturalized citizen. Six months later after U.S. citizenship was granted, Saadi moved to Albuquerque, New Mexico and formed the Askari Mosque. "That's about all I've got Tony," stated Special Agent Perez.

"Thanks Manny, stay in touch," replied Tony.

Tony walked over to Sharon who was sitting at a computer terminal. Deep in thought she was unaware of his presence.

"What are you coming up with Shar?"

Sharon responded, "Born in Palestine in June, 1954. Immigrated to the U.S. in August, 1994, resided in Detroit until January 2000, at which time he moved to Albuquerque and opened the Askari Mosque sometime in 2001. Also, and this is where it gets interesting, he published several articles during the last two years supporting the Islamic radicalization movements in Palestine and the West Bank."

"So what does that tell us?"

"It tells us that the Imam is at least 'sympathetic' to radical Islam," Sharon announced.

Stopping back at Tony's to pick up a long sleeve blouse for Sharon; Tony suggested that they eat lunch before facing the Imam again.

CHAPTER 26

"**Ever been to** the 'Owl Café,'" queried Tony.

"Sounds like some kinda law enforcement hangout," quipped Sharon.

"No it's actually serves the very best 'green chili cheeseburger' in town."

Moments later they arrived at brown stucco structure, with the stylized outline of an "owl" carved into roof.

"It looks like a diner," opined Sharon as a waitress showed them to a table.

The loquacious server handed them a menu, as Sharon asked, "What's good?"

"I told you Shar, you have to order the green chili cheeseburger!"

Less than five minutes passed, and the waitress returned with their plates. A hefty hamburger, dripping in cheese along with "too many" fries were deposited in front of them.

"Dig in," demanded Tony.

Forty minutes later, walking back to their car Sharon remarked, "I don't think I can eat for a week, with all that food."

"Told you," smiled Tony.

Ten minutes driving time had returned them back in front of the mosque.

As they departed the vehicle they encountered an overwhelming chanting sound.

Tony asked, "What's that bizarre noise, it sounds like a bee hive on steroids?"

"Prayer time," Sharon explained. "Faithful Moslems observe prayer, five times per day. This is probably (glancing at her watch), 'Zuhr.' We need to stay put until they're finished. It should not be that long."

Seven minutes passed, and the same group of men which they encountered earlier in the morning appeared back on the front patio. As before, Tony approached the men, however, this time Sharon stayed glued to his backside.

"Hello," Tony shouted, "I'm looking for Imam Saadi."

Again, the cluster of men did not move. After a few moments of painful stares, the Imam materialized in the doorway.

"I expected you earlier," Saadi muttered.

"We were busy," recited Tony

"So what so important that you wish to converse with me?" inquired the Imam.

"Well, we would like this to be a private conversation Imam," relayed Tony.

Wrinkling his forehead, the supercilious Imam ushered Tony and Sharon into the buildings foyer. Just inside the foyer, Tony and Sharon were led through a large room dominated by several dozen small, woven wool rugs. The rugs were laid out facing the East. Except for the colorful miniature carpets, the room was empty. The Imam gingerly stepped through the room and advanced toward the rear of the building. There were three doorways in the rear, and the Imam opened a door to the left which revealed a vast room. Inside the space was enormous table, which appeared to serve as the Imam's desk. On the table was a Dell computer, several worn copies of the Qur'an, and stacks of documents and files. The Imam took a seat at a hefty chair facing the table. Since no other chairs were in the room, Tony and Sharon stood facing the Imam.

After what seemed like several minutes, the Imam expelled an exaggerated breath of air and extended his arms in front of him. "So what is the purpose of your visit?" the Imam exclaimed.

"I am Special Agent Garza with the Federal Bureau of Investigation, and this is Miss Sharon Martinez with the Department of Homeland Security." Tony then opened up his FBI credentials and abruptly flashed them towards Imam Saadi.

"During the last few days a number of criminal activities— terrorist activities have occurred. We have reason to believe these terrorist acts were committed by members of this mosque."

The Imam folded his hands together and pursing his lips, intoned, "That's utter nonsense. My worshippers would not be a party to such behavior."

"Well Imam Saadi, eight men have been arrested so far, and three suspects are still at large. The men that are being held have admitted to being active members of your mosque. What do you say to that?"

"Ridiculous!" shouted the Imam.

"Imam Saadi, I need to inform you that any complicit behavior on your part is subject federal prosecution. Good day, Imam."

CHAPTER 27

YOUSEF KHAN ARRIVED at the Albuquerque Greyhound Bus terminal late in the evening. His plan was to walk the roughly two miles to his reach his destination. After less than forty minutes Khan scanned the block leading to the Askari Mosque. Careful to look as if he was ambling about on an evening stroll, he wanted to ensure that no law enforcement officials were waiting for him. Looking toward the front of the mosque, it appeared that the last prayer call (Isha) had ended just minutes before. Some of the elders were smoking cigarettes and chatting in hushed tones on the portico.

Circling the block, Yousef scanned the rear of the mosque. Acting deliberate, he made his way down the alleyway behind and to the right of the mosque. Yousef paused, trying to discern movement in the darkness. Satisfied that no one was about, he quickly climbed over the rusted chain-linked fence and darted into one of the dilapidated out- buildings. Feeling his way in the pitch-black structure, he fingered an old cot. He opened the makeshift bed, and carefully set his package of nitro-methane underneath the cot. He mentally reviewed his actions during the last two days and reaffirmed his determination for his mission. "I will show the world," he whispered to himself. Staring into darkness, his body constricted slightly as his countenance took on a steadfast resolve.

Exhausted he lay down to sleep.

Before Yousef closed his eyes he thought of the kind lady on the bus. "She is a sign," he reflected. "I will transform my identity tomorrow. I will become Latino." Throughout the night, he dreamt of altering his persona.

"Insha'Allah," sighed Yousef.

CHAPTER 28

RISING AT DAWN, Yousef peered out into the early morning light. Hiking to the university, he surveyed the countless bicycle racks. Spying an unattended mountain bike, he casually pulled it from the stand and drove off.

Yousef peddled down Central Avenue, east toward the town of Edgewood, New Mexico.

Months earlier while hiking in the mountains, Yousef noticed some road construction and related demolition work taking place in the area. Demolition crews were working to widen interstate 40 as it sliced through mountains. At last he approached a turnoff with a bright orange sign that read, "Blasting—Stay Out." He got off the bicycle and laid it next to a huge coniferous tree.

The area was barricaded with wire rope and fencing to discourage admittance. He could observe several construction workers inside the fenced off area. A large dump truck carrying a load of boulders was slowly moving toward a gated region. A guard wearing a yellow vest advanced toward the gate to allow the truck to pass through. After the truck left, Yousef came up to guard and asked if he could speak to the foreman. The guard ushered Yousef to a dented aluminum trailer.

The guard knocked on the trailer door, then opened it. He looked in, and shouted, "Boss, this guy wants to speak with you."

A massive man wearing a steel construction helmet appeared in the doorway of the trailer. "What can I do for you young man," bellowed the foreman.

Yousef meekly asked the foreman if he could speak with him for a minute.

"Come on in!" barked the foreman, as Yousef entered the small trailer.

"Sir, my name is Juan Veldez," Yousef lied. "I'm an engineering student at UNM, and am graduating next spring. I'm considering employment in road construction when I graduate, and would like see what you do. I'm willing to work for free and assist you anyway I can. Could I please work with you for a few days until my semester begins in two weeks?"

The beefy foreman smiled and growled, "Work for free 'coffee man?'"

Yousef did not understand the bulky foreman's reference to the Columbian Coffee commercial.

"Yes sir, I will work very hard for you without pay."

"Well that's an offer I can't refuse. Coffee man, why don't you start by making some coffee?"

"Okay," Yousef nodded politely and went about making coffee in the confined trailer.

After Yousef finished brewing the coffee in an enormous percolator, the large foreman looked over at Yousef.

"Juan please don't take offense, but you don't look old enough to be out of high school yet."

Yousef just smiled and said, "I'm just here to learn."

By early afternoon, Yousef had made two more pots of coffee, swept out the trailer, and followed the burly foreman throughout the construction site.

At four o'clock in the afternoon the foreman declared, "Well that's it for today Juan. Thanks for all your work. Are you sure you want to try this again in the morning?"

"Yes sir, I've discovered a lot already, and I'll be here first thing in morning." Yousef then boarded his pilfered bike and rode down the mountain road.

CHAPTER 29

THE NEXT DAY Tony and Sharon occupied their time trying to figure out the best way to track down the three remaining alleged terrorists. They made a trip back to the university's Registrar's office to get copies of the suspect's student identification cards. Upon receipt, they noticed that in all three of the remaining suspects ID pictures—all had facial hair and long locks. Both Tony and Sharon remembered when they had interviewed the suspects that were being held in custody, that all of the young men had been clean shaven with short hair.

"I'll bet they shaved to help disguise their Pakistani identity," stated Tony.

"I won't take that bet, Tony. Doesn't the FBI have a computer simulation that can take the photos from their IDs and alter them, making them clean shaven?"

"We do Shar, but I have to get the pictures back to headquarters, and it might take a couple of days."

"At least it's a start. How do we proceed in the mean time?" asked Sharon.

"Well, the Imam still looks connected to me. We could stakeout his mosque, and see what happens. I just don't want to waste valuable time on surveillance."

Sharon accompanied Tony back to his office where he faxed the three student IDs to the FBI laboratory in Quantico, Virginia. Next Tony met with the Joint Terrorism Task Force personnel where he briefed the team leaders on where he was at with his part of the investigation. He detailed his plan to stakeout the mosque and took input from his supervisor to ensure a coordinated law enforcement effort.

After the meeting Sharon called her supervisor at the Santa Fe fusion center. Referring to her notes, she presented the day's highlights to him. After exchanging a few questions and answers, she hung up the phone and joined Tony in his cubicle.

CHAPTER 30

IN AN EFFORT to transform Yousef Khan the Pakistani into Juan Veldez the Latino, Khan decided to further enhance his appearance and mannerisms by spending some time in Albuquerque's ethnic neighborhoods.

Yousef's native language was Punjabi, and he had mastered English in school. In addition he spoke Urdu, Farsi, and some Arabic, which he picked up through his religious training. Yousef excelled at languages, so picking up the idioms of the Spanish language had been relatively easy.

Early the next morning Yousef once again used his pilfered bicycle to travel to the highway construction site in Edgewood, New Mexico. As he greeted the foreman, the hefty man grinned and remarked, "I'm so happy you returned for another day Juan."

Yousef busied himself making coffee and tidying up the construction trailer. After some time the burly foreman announced, "Juan, I've got a special treat for you today. We're blowing some rock, and you get to witness the ground moving under your feet."

A few minutes later Juan and the foreman were driving down an unpaved road to the demolition site. They pulled in front of a battered construction trailer marked "Ordnance" in large red letters. Juan followed behind the foreman as he entered the trailer. Three huge men in bib overalls and wearing red hardhats were peering over a map and discussing the day's events. The largest of the men looked up as Juan and the foreman entered.

"Boys meet Juan, my little helper," announced the foreman.

The large ordnance man with a weathered face and straw colored hair stepped forward and held out his hand. "The boss tells us you want to be a demolition engineer, Juan," stated the man.

"That's right sir," replied Juan, shaking the man's enormous hand.

"They call me 'Red,'" stated the large man.

Then Red asked Juan to follow him to his command vehicle to observe the demolition site. "Juan, once we get to the site, please do not wander off and don't touch anything." Juan nodded in agreement.

Upon their arrival at the site, Red instructed Juan to stay close to him. He went on to explain and show Juan the boreholes that were drilled into the granite shelf the previous day. He further clarified that today his ordnance men would wrap detonating cord or det-cord around sausage shaped tubes called "chubs." The det-cord would extend from the borehole where a blasting cap would be attached. The blasting cap would be set off by an electrical wire running several hundred yards from the detonation site. He further clarified that the number of boreholes times the explosive weight in each hole determined the actual safe distance from the detonation.

"Safety is our number one concern in this operation," declared the ordnance man. "I'll let you see my ordnance crew prepare one hole, and then were out of here."

Juan observed with rapt attention as a demolition technician prepared a hole. Then Red led Juan, to what appeared to be a distance of almost three quarters of mile away.

"I was hoping to see the blast," pleaded Juan. "Don't worry Juan, your going to see and feel the explosion as soon as my men finish up."

A little over two hours later Juan was drinking coffee with Red and getting an overview of the planned demolition. As Red's crew returned to the trailer, Red instructed Juan as to how they checked the continuity of the wire circuit as he attached the lead wires to a power box. Next Red flipped a toggle switch which activated an ear shattering siren. Red explained the siren was to alert all personnel that an explosion was imminent.

"Okay Juan, new guy gets to set off the explosives," announced Red. "Yell '*fire in the hole*' and depress the red button."

Juan did as he was told, but initially nothing happened. Juan started to depress the button a second time when Red shouted for him to be patient. Two seconds later, a tremendous explosion was heard followed by a violent shaking of the trailer when the blast wave hit. Juan first thought that something had gone wrong and that trailer would be damaged in the blast. Red and his ordnance crew laughed as they observed Juan's obvious discomfort. Moments passed and Red told Juan to follow him outside the trailer. Once outside Red pointed to the giant plume on the horizon.

"¡Mierda!" Juan exclaimed in Spanish.

Chapter 31

SA Garza and Sharon Martinez obtained simulated photographs of the three outstanding, alleged terrorists. The university identification pictures were altered utilizing a FBI laboratory "Photoshop" enhancement. The resulting images removed the suspect's facial hair and gave them shorter hairstyles.

Tony and Sharon had been conducting a surveillance of the Imam's mosque for the past two days. So far nothing had occurred that seemed unusual or suspicious. They assumed that since the fugitives could not return to the university, the only possible nexus would be the Imam at the mosque.

So far nothing useful had turned up from the campus police, immigration authorities, or subsequent interviews with the eight other Pakistani students currently being detained.

With time on their hands, SA Garza and Sharon Martinez sat for hours in Tony's government vehicle and talked. They had the obvious bond with the prevailing notion of catching the bad guys, but both Tony and Sharon discovered more about each other, their backgrounds, goals and desires, likes and dislikes.

Sharon had shared with Tony that she grown up in the small city of Farmington, New Mexico. Her mother was a traditional Hispanic homemaker, staying home and caring for Sharon's six siblings while her father labored as a pipe fitter at a natural gas conglomerate. Being the eldest child, Sharon helped her mother with family chores and watching over her younger brothers and sisters. She excelled academically in high school and graduated with honors. She applied and received a full scholarship at American University in Washington D.C. Sharon obtained a bachelor degree in International Studies, and continued on to get a master's degree in Foreign Security. Upon completion of her education, Sharon obtained her first real job as an intelligence analyst with the State Department.

Working with the State Department, Sharon enjoyed the bustle of working and living in the nation's capital. However, after three years, Sharon longed to be closer to her family. She applied for, and was accepted to her current position with the newly established Department of Homeland Security in the geographically separated office in Santa Fe.

Tony tended to be more guarded in discussing his personal life. But with Sharon, he uncharacteristically found himself giving out more information about himself that few people knew.

Anthony Garza was raised in Tucson, Arizona. His father was a homicide detective with the Tucson Police Department and his mother was employed as a registered nurse with the county. An only child, Tony was a standout athlete in high school and lettered in football and baseball. Tony attended Arizona State University, where he was a walk-on running back for the football team. Playing third string, Tony typically saw playing time during the second half of most of the team's games. That was until the third game of the season during his senior year, when a massive defensive lineman managed to crush his left knee which terminated his college football career. Tony went on to graduate in the spring with a criminal justice degree.

With help from his father, Tony was offered a position with the Tucson Police Department shortly after graduating. Tony and his girlfriend and constant companion during his junior and senior year, decided somewhat abruptly, to get married after Tony had been on the police force for somewhat less than one year.

The marriage lasted the better part of two years. His wife unexpectedly announced, "that the fire had gone out," and she wanted a divorce. Tony, caught off guard, went from shock, disbelief, to mild depression. After the divorce, and to deal with his grief, Tony decided to move on with his life and applied as a special agent with the FBI. Several months went by, when Tony received a letter notifying him that had been accepted to the FBI. After twenty weeks of training at Quantico, Tony's first posting was with the FBI field office in Dallas, Texas. Tony stayed in Texas for five years and eventually put in for an opening at Albuquerque field office.

Throughout the evening Sharon and Tony shared stories, insights, and musings.

CHAPTER 32

YOUSEF PROMISED TO meet Red, the ordnance team chief at daybreak early the next morning. Red informed Juan that he would be working at his side inspecting, transporting, loading, and firing explosives. "Juan," said Red, "the only way you really get to experience being a demolition engineer is to live it. The work day is often times long, the work tedious, and it is dangerous. But I would not do anything else, blasting rock is my life."

Juan met Red as he entered the construction site just before sunrise. After parking his personal truck, Red jumped into the battered company truck and motioned for Juan to join him. Arriving at the "Ordnance" trailer a few minutes later, Red again told Juan to stay by his side. "Juan, why don't you make some coffee—then we can go over the day's events before the rest of the crew show up."

As they drank their first cup of coffee, Red showed Juan how he used the map to detail the day's work plan. The first map Red laid out was a topographic map. "Juan," as Red pointed to the map, "the brown lines on the map represent contours or points of elevation. When the lines are close together, they represent a steep slope and the lines far apart represent a gradual slope. Then the civil engineers survey the actual points and produce this blue line map. This map shows the projected road design and location. From this blue line map, I plug everything into my computer, and come up with the number, distance, diameter, and depth of boreholes required."

"So it's a CADM program?" inquired Juan.

"Yes son, that's correct," nodded Red.

Red went on to explain, "From there, the boreholes are plotted and, then printed on the diagram that we're looking at. The drillers use this chart to drill their holes and we use it to plan how much, and where the explosives go."

Juan nodded indicating that he understood.

"When you finish your coffee Juan, we're going out to scope out the holes that were drilled yesterday."

"I'm ready sir," grinned Juan.

After a careful examination of the demo site, Red informed Juan that it was the ordnance chief's responsibility to determine the optimum points of ingress and egress for the transport of the explosives for his crew. He explained to Juan how important it was to have a well thought-out plan—and that vigilance and attention to detail were vital to have a safe and successful operation.

"Again Juan, safety is always paramount."

When they returned to the ordnance trailer the rest of Red's crew had arrived, Red got on the telephone and ordered delivery of the explosives from a location elsewhere on the construction site.

"Juan all of us will meet the explosives truck down near the boreholes. We'll all unload the truck until the chubs are laid out, mated with the det-cord, and loaded. Once we begin this operation, we do not stop until we are finished. Are you up for it?"

"Yes sir," Juan replied.

When the explosives truck arrived, the ordnance crew carefully picked up the chubs and laid them near the boreholes where they would eventually be loaded. Based on the height of the granite shelf, Red told the members of his crew to lay out six chubs per hole. The unloading of the chubs took the crew in excess of an hour. Next Red pulled two large spoils of det-cord off of the truck. Finally Red picked up a wooden box marked detonators and set it next to a large boulder. Red instructed the driver to vacate the area, as the crew began cutting, wrapping, and loading the explosives.

Juan stayed next to Red as Red showed him how to cut the det-cord to a predetermined length. Then Red arranged the chubs so that they remained in contact with each other once the det-cord was fastened. And finally, Red showed Juan how to load each continuous mass into the individual boreholes. This process took over three hours. Red went on to explain to Juan that all of the cords which now extended out of the holes had to be tied-in together. To accomplish this, a member of crew unwound a long piece of cut det-cord and attached it to the det-cord that extended from the two boreholes which were the greatest distance apart.

"This piece of detonation cord is called the 'ring-main,'" stated Red, "all the other pieces will be tied into it."

Next Red, with Juan at his side went from hole to hole to inspect the completed work. "Now we are ready for the caps, Juan," recited Red, "can you go up by that large rock and bring me that red box? Please be very careful because it contains blasting caps."

Juan retrieved the box. Red opened the box and showed Juan the contents. "Juan, these are blasting caps. Some folks refer to them as detonators. These will initiate the det-cord which will set off the main charge. Blasting caps are extremely sensitive to heat, shock, friction, or any kind of abuse. That is why we take great care in how we handle them."

Red pulled out three caps from the box and instructed Juan to return the box to his pickup truck. Juan carried the box back to Red's truck. As he carefully lowered the box into the truck bed, he looked surreptitiously about and realized that he out of sight of Red and his crew. He opened the lid of the box and withdrew two blasting caps. Carefully wrapping the caps in a discarded rag, Juan furtively pocketed his pilfered treasure.

When Juan returned, Red continued to instruct him on the use of the blasting caps. "Juan," advised Red, "the wires extending from the caps are called 'leg wires.' As you can see the wires are shunted together to prevent them from getting a stray voltage and setting off the cap. You should always point the cap away from you when working with it, like this."

Pulling off the shunt and separating the wires, Red showed him how to check the electrical continuity with his blast meter. Then, Red re-shunted the leg wires and demonstrated how to tape the caps to the ring-main det-cord. Finally, Red unrolled a large spoil of lamp cord. Red shunted one end of the lamp cord and attached the other end to the leg wires of the detonators and yelled for his crew to move out.

As they walked from the area, Juan asked Red why they were using three blasting caps to set of the explosives.

"Just as a redundancy Juan, good question. In theory you need just one cap to make this sucker work."

Red told his crew to finish stringing the lamp cord toward the ordnance trailer as he and Juan drove back to the trailer in Red's pickup.

Thirty minutes later Juan along with Red and his crew were back in the trailer. Red flipped the siren to announce forthcoming detonation. "Juan, you do the honors," shouted Red.

"Fire in the hole," screamed Juan, as he depressed the red button.

CHAPTER 33

AFTER TWO DAYS of sitting in his government issued black Suburban, both SA Garza and Sharon were growing impatient. Finally, Garza blurted, "Maybe we are attacking this all wrong. We've been monitoring the mosque from the front for two days, but if someone wasn't suppose to be here, perhaps they wouldn't come in from the front. If they were trying to conceal themselves, they might be sneaking in from the rear. What do you think Shar?"

"At this point we have nothing to lose."

Pulling Tony's car to the rear and down the block from the mosque, Tony and Sharon had a good view of the property line in back of the mosque. He suggested that Sharon try to get some sleep while he maintained observation of the grounds.

Shortly after daylight Sharon awoke with a start, finding Tony chuckling and grinning widely to himself.

"What's so funny ?"

Tony responded, "I just heard a funny story on the radio."

Tony began, "After a severe bombing campaign in Pakistan, Osama Bin Laden was killed and arrived at the 'pearly gates.' There, he is greeted by George Washington."

"How dare you attack the nation I helped conceive!" yells Mr. Washington, slapping Osama in the face.

Patrick Henry comes up from behind, "You wanted to end the Americans' liberty, so they gave you death!" Patrick Henry punches Osama on the nose.

James Madison comes up next, and says, "This is why I allowed the Federal government to provide for the common defense!" as he kicks Osama in the groin.

Osama is subject to similar beatings from James Monroe, Thomas Jefferson along with sixty-six 18th century American revolutionary heroes, who hurl him back toward the gate where he is to be judged.

As Osama awaits his journey to his final destination, he screams, "This is not what I was promised!"

An angel replies, "I told you there would be 72 Virginians waiting for you. What did you think I said?"

Sharon laughed spontaneously and responded, "I got one for you. Why doesn't the Taliban have drivers ed and sex ed classes on the same day?"

Tony smiling, shook his head.

"Because the camels can't handle it," muttered Sharon.

Both Tony and Sharon erupted in laughter.

"Well Tony, I've finally decided you do have a sense of humor."

CHAPTER 34

YOUSEF FINGERED THE stolen blasting caps as he peddled his bike back into town. He had purchased the nitro-methane and pilfered the blasting caps in accordance with his dream on the bus returning from Las Vegas. He truly believed that this was a special spiritual direction from Allah. Although, he had not worked out all of the specifics of his plan, Yousef felt confident that additional guidance would be forthcoming.

As Yousef returned to mosque, he happened to noticed a black SUV parked several meters away from the front entrance. The vehicle appeared to have two occupants lingering in the front seats. He was immediately suspicious of the vehicle's presence, and decided that perhaps he should look for a new lair in which to conceal himself. Yousef secreted his bicycle a few blocks away and returned to the outbuilding which he had hidden the fuel oil.

As he snuck over the fence to the rear of mosque, he was surprised to encounter the Imam. The Imam greeted Yousef warmly.

"Masa'ul khayr, Yousef (Good evening)," whispered the Imam.

"Assalaam Alaikum (Peace be upon you)," replied Yousef.

Yousef updated the Imam of his travails during the last five days.

The Imam informed Yousef that law enforcement agents have made inquiries about him and that the "infidels had soiled the mosque with their presence."

Yousef mentioned that he was on another "mission" from Allah, and that he would seek refuge elsewhere. The Imam told Yousef to wait a moment while he made an inquiry within the mosque. Minutes went by and finally the Imam returned. He handed Yousef a folded piece of paper. Yousef opened the paper to reveal a name, address, and directions. Yousef nodded politely.

The Imam recited, "Assalaam Alaikum, Yousef."

"Wa Alaikum assalaam," replied Yousef.

He retrieved his hidden bottle of fuel oil, and walked down the block to reclaim his bicycle.

CHAPTER 35

SHARON MARTINEZ WATCHED intently from SA Garza's vehicle, as Garza walked to a nearby Central avenue restaurant to buy breakfast burritos. Martinez observed some outside activity following the Morning Prayer at the mosque. The Imam appeared in the rear of mosque engaged in an animated conversation with two scruffy looking elders. Amid hand waving, pointing, and other gesticulation, the Imam appeared agitated about something. Moments later additional men appeared in the rear courtyard. Sharon gasped as she observed two younger males, clean shaven in western dress standing in the middle of the group.

Minutes later Tony appeared, opened the drivers door and began to hand out their breakfast meals.

"Hold on, we might have something here!" grunted Sharon. "See the two young men inside the group."

Tony looked on for brief time while making a quick scan of the student suspects' composite photos. "Looks like two of em," suggested Tony. "I wonder where little Joe might be?"

Tony called for Albuquerque Police backup. He instructed the dispatcher to have the responding officer's rendezvous three blocks up from the mosque, with no sirens. Tony informed the dispatcher that he would meet the officers and plan their "probable cause" takedown.

Ten minutes had passed, with the Imam and his group still in the courtyard. Tony told Sharon to stay in the car as he departed to meet with the APD officers. When Tony met up with the police, five cruisers had arrived on scene with two policemen assigned to each car. Tony asked for all of the responders to gather around so he could go over a quick plan of attack. He introduced himself, and then gave the officers a brief overview of the situation, and informed them about the alleged suspects.

Tony pulled out a sheet of notebook paper and sketched out a rough description of mosque and outbuildings. He told the officers that he along with three police officers would be entering through the front, with the remaining policemen covering the rear and the outer perimeter. "I want this to be safe, quick, and productive," said Tony, "Anybody have any questions before we move out?"

CHAPTER 36

YOUSEF'S NEW RESIDENCE was in a storage shed of a prominent Albuquerque Muslim resident. He had ridden his bike to Glenwood Hills. Glenwood Hills is an upper middle class neighborhood located in the Northeast Albuquerque foothills. The locale seemed ideal for Yousef as it took him outside of the downtown university area, and put him in a quiet upscale locality. The owner of the home was employed as a senior engineer for Sandia National Laboratory and remained a devout Muslim with links to the Imam Saadi and the Askari Mosque.

As Yousef awoke to the bright sunny day, he remembered his dream from the night before. In the dream, he was instructed to conduct research once again on a Jihadist website in order to prepare his special gift for the American infidels. As Yousef wandered outside of his shed, he discovered that his new dwelling backed up to a forest preserve. The preserve had foot trails that led into and up through the mountain range surrounding the Northern boundary of the city. As Yousef gazed at the rugged landscape, the home's owner appeared and greeted him warmly.

"Sabah al khair (good morning) Yousef," welcomed the owner of the home. He then ushered Yousef to a wrought iron table where he laid down a tray bearing small plates of naan flat bread, feta cheese, dates, black olives, an herb omelet, and gahwa (coffee). The owner then instructed Yousef to enjoy his breakfast. He then stated that he was leaving for work and returning in the early evening. "If there is anything you need Yousef, please let me know," whispered the man.

Yousef was overcome with the beautiful sight and aromatic smell of the food left before him. Since he hadn't eaten a full meal in nearly a week, he ate ravenously.

CHAPTER 37

SA GARZA CAUTIOUSLY approached the front of the mosque with two Albuquerque policemen to his rear. With his right hand on his holstered weapon, he rapped firmly with his left hand against the solid core front door. He waited for a few moments and knocked again this time shouting, "FBI, open up!"

Again, waiting for a few moments, he then repeated the process. Finally the door opened, and the Imam appeared. "Well, what brings you here again," grunted the Imam.

Garza stated firmly, "we have reason to believe that you are harboring suspect terrorists."

"That's ridiculous," replied the Imam.

Just then a loud commotion could be heard in the rear of the mosque. "Everyone down, and put your hands behind your back," commanded a stern voice.

Garza rushed past the Imam with the two policemen in tow. In the rear yard, five of Albuquerque's finest had four elders and the two young males lying on the sandy ground with their hands clasp behind them.

"The two males attempted to escape as they heard 'FBI, open up,'" explained a young patrolman. "We caught them as they hopped over the chain link fence."

"Cuff em!" instructed Garza.

Garza led the Imam back into the mosque and into the Imam's private office. "Sit!" commanded Garza. "Okay Imam Saadi, we can do this the easy way—or we can do it the hard way. I can have you indicted for harboring fugitive terrorists or you can tell me the whereabouts of Yousef Khan, right now!"

"I do not know where Yousef Khan is, I am not his keeper," mumbled the arrogant Imam.

"Well you did know where two student fugitives were!" barked Garza.

"They just showed up early this morning, I was getting ready to notify the authorities," muttered the Imam.

"Bullshit!" replied Garza.

Garza again walked to the rear of the mosque where the APD officers had the two young suspects in custody in back of one their patrol cars. Both students were crying uncontrollably and chanting some strange phase. "Take them in and lock em up," commanded Garza. He then went to each patrolman and thanked them for all their help.

Sharon was standing next to the back fence watching all the activity. Tony strolled over to Sharon and uttered, "Well two more down, and one to go. Let's get some chow."

"We still have the burritos you bought Tony."

Tony rejoined, "I'd suggest we get a hot sit-down breakfast. After that I need to get some sleep."

CHAPTER 38

AFTER FINISHING HIS generous breakfast, Yousef Khan hiked along the deserted foothills. The bright sun, majestic mountains, and gentle breeze had a calming affect on him that he had not experienced in many days. He wandered along the desert trails ruminating about his mission.

Yousef thought back over the last few days. He pondered his recent trip to the decadent, indulgent city of Las Vegas; the detailed preparation, the planning and execution of his assignment, and ultimate outcome. He resolved that his new mission would be even more successful. He was determined that with Allah's help, he would be victorious. Yousef meandered among the barren landscape throughout the morning, becoming ever more confident of his upcoming task.

Returning to his surreptitious shed just after noon, Yousef rested. He quickly was fast asleep and began dreaming of his destiny. In the early afternoon, after sleeping for almost four hours, he awoke feeling refreshed and more driven. He decided to wander around his neighborhood and experience his new locale. He walked over to Tramway boulevard and discovered a public library. He drifted into the library appearing much like the library's other visitors. He found a vacant computer carrel, and sat down in front of the workstation.

As he was surfing the web, he readily discovered that all his young colleagues had been apprehended and were presently awaiting prosecution for the intentional initiation of pyrotechnic devices in several states. Several headlines captivated Yousef's attention to include: *Islamic Terrorists Destroy America's Virgin Forests, Deliberate Acts of Terror Prompts Special Senate Inquiry, Radical Muslim Group Investigated—Presumed Leader Still at Large, POTUS Urges Restraint Amid Public Outrage, Nevada Explosion Creates Environmental Tragedy.* Yousef read through the myriad of media reports, essays, and commentary. At 9:45 that evening, a librarian came by and told him that the library was closing in fifteen minutes. As he left the library, his mind was racing. He tried to comprehend the enormity of what he had perpetrated and rationalize his next actions.

Yousef was also alerted to the fact that he was wanted by the authorities as a "subject of interest" for the explosive detonation at the Nevada military base. He walked swiftly back to his hideaway, where his mind raced. . "Insha'Allah," recited Yousef.

Chapter 39

"**Are you hungry** Sharon?" Tony asked as they were driving to a restaurant.

"Famished," replied Sharon.

"Then I've got the ideal place."

Tony drove down Central avenue took a left at Broadway boulevard, and pulled into the parking lot of "Grandma's K & I Diner." "What's this?" asked Sharon.

"You'll see," replied Tony grinning.

As they entered the restaurant Sharon remarked, "It looks like something out of the 1950's."

As they were seated Tony suggested, "I'll order for both of us."

"Okay," Sharon replied shaking her head.

A middle aged waitress appeared and asked, "Hi ya sugar, what can I get ya?"

"The lady will have a 'Travis' and I'll have a 'Half Travis,'" announced Tony.

As the friendly waitress departed, Sharon asked, "What's a Travis, Tony?"

"You'll see," Tony smirked.

After a few minutes of lighthearted discussion, the waitress appeared with an enormous platter of food. "Here honey," as she placed the steaming serving dish in front of Sharon. The waitress giggled as she served Tony. Tony's dish was large, but paled in comparison to Sharon's salver.

"Okay, so what's this?

"It's your 'Travis,' Sharon, eat and enjoy. You said you were hungry."

"What is it?"

"The 'Travis' is a meat and bean burrito, smothered with cheese and chili, then piled high with French fries. Enjoy!"

Midway through their meal, Tony noticed that Sharon had dribbled some cheese sauce on the bottom left of her chin. "Here," said Tony, "let me get this for you." Tony folded his napkin and gently wiped her chin.

"Thank you kind sir," smiled Sharon.

One hour and twenty minutes later, Tony had mostly consumed his plate of food. Sharon's platter looked only partially nibbled on. "I'm done Tony; I can not eat another bite."

As they drove out of the parking space, Tony announced, "I'm dead to the world, I really need to get some shuteye."

Chapter 40

When Yousef awoke at sunrise, he was again greeted by the home's owner who again had prepared a magnificent breakfast of various fruits, eggs, and coffee. The owner wished Yousef well, and left for work. Yousef savored his meal while mentally planning his day.

After consuming his meal, he walked to a nearby gas station. Inside the gas station, Yousef meticulously explored the various items for sale. Among the sundry objects such as foodstuffs, tobacco products, and vehicle maintenance merchandise, he spotted an aisle that normally a tourist would make use of. Shelves containing 'Albuquerque Balloon Fiesta 2002' tee-shirts, baseball caps with logos featuring the 'Albuquerque Isotopes,' 'UNM Lobos,' and 'Land of Enchantment' lined the walkway. Yousef selected two tee-shirts, and a red Lobos ball cap. After making his purchase, He strolled outside and adjusted the ball cap so that it fitted his small head. When he put it on, he wore the cap's bill toward the rear. This affectation was to further enhance his disguise.

Yousef wandered aimlessly for over an hour until the branch library opened. This was the same library that he had visited the day before. Entering the library he selected the same computer carrel that he had previously occupied. For the next several hours he busied himself pouring over many of the same news articles that he had perused earlier. As early evening approached, a librarian strolled by, and asked him what he was researching.

"I'm doing a paper for school," explained Yousef, affecting a slight Spanish accent.

"Well, you're certainly dedicated," remarked the friendly librarian.

CHAPTER 41

SPECIAL AGENT GARZA and Sharon Martinez slept soundly throughout the night at Garza's home in Northwest Albuquerque. When Sharon awoke at 7:30 A.M., she found Tony busy at his laptop computer at the kitchen table.

"Good morning, sleepy head," murmured Garza.

"Morning Tony, what time did you get up?"

"Bout two hours ago. Coffee?"

"Sure, want me to fix breakfast?"

"Sounds great, let me finish up this report and I'll help you."

As they were finishing their breakfast of scrambled eggs, bacon, and toast, Tony mentioned to Sharon that the DOJ was preparing charges to be brought against Imam Saadi.

"If the Albuquerque federal prosecutor can put some heat on the Imam, we might get him to tell us what he knows about Yousef Khan."

"What if he doesn't know anything?" asked Sharon.

"Well my gut instinct is that he does know something. How involved he was with what Khan was up to remains to be seen. At any rate what other avenue do we have to pursue?"

"I'm with you Tony."

"For now we've requested subpoenas for the Imam's phone records and I've requested to get his phone tapped."

"So what do we do now, Tony?" asked Sharon.

"We wait." replied Tony, impatiently tapping his fingers on the kitchen table.

CHAPTER 42

YOUSEF RETURNED TO his hideaway later that evening. He was tired amid the strain of reading most of the day at the library, and quickly fell to sleep after coming in contact with his bed.

Again, in the morning he rose early and again was greeted by the property owner. The owner had a superb breakfast laid out but this time sat with Yousef as Yousef ate.

"What are your plans on this fine day Yousef?" inquired the owner.

"I think I will visit the library and then go for a hike. I would again like to thank you for your accommodations."

"No problem," said the owner, "whatever you need please let me know." With that, the owner stood up, and left Yousef to finish his meal.

Stretching, Yousef tramped into the trail behind the house toward the mountains. Hiking allowed him to be at peace with himself and to clearly focus on his ultimate mission. As he crested the top of a large granite outcropping, he looked back and down toward the city. Yousef had a spectacular view of the city and he took a moment to admire the panoramic setting. The vista filled him with a sense of omnipotence. He trekked further, and the higher he ventured in elevation, the more it buoyed his confidence.

Just before noon, he returned to his shed, where he changed into one of the tee-shirts along with the red ball cap, that he had purchased the day before. He leisurely strolled back to the library. Using the same computer, he searched the internet for some of the Jihadist's websites that he had frequented several months earlier. Finding what he was looking for, he made copious notes. He was as meticulous doing research as he was in using his research to execute his plan.

He returned to his dwelling just after nightfall. As with the previous two nights he was asleep soon after his head hit his bed. This night however, Yousef had another dream. Armed with information from his day of study coupled with his dream, a plan was slowly starting to develop.

Chapter 43

Special Agent Garza awoke early to meet with his supervisor at the field office in Albuquerque. Supervisory Special Agent Joseph Burris was a large man with an infectious sense of humor, insatiable appetite, and down to earth manner.

"Well Tony, late last night we received the Attorney General's go ahead with the subpoena for Imam Saadi. We also got permission to access his phone records and monitor his calls. All this should be in place later this afternoon. As we discussed yesterday, we are getting a tremendous amount of pressure from headquarters and everywhere else. I'll do my best to keep the heat off of you, and let you do your job."

"Thanks Joe. I really think if we sweat the Imam a bit, he'll spill what he knows. At any rate, he is the only lead we have right now, as the rest of the students aren't talking much and I don't believe they were told much concerning Khan's plans," replied Garza.

"Now Tony, tell daddy what's going on between you and the lady from Homeland Security?"

"Not much to tell Joe. Sharon is an intel analyst that I met through the Santa Fe fusion office. She brings a new perspective outside of law enforcement."

"You really should be working with our field intel folks, don't you think Tony?'

"Well Joe, I really like working by myself, and Sharon helps me but stays out of the way."

"Okay Tony, just be careful, stay safe—and understand we're getting loads of attention with this one."

"You got it boss," said Tony as he departed his office.

As Tony returned to his condo, Sharon was busy doing laundry and making sandwiches for lunch.

"What did your boss have to say Tony?" inquired Sharon.

"Well the AG's pressing forward on the Imam. And we should have the phone monitors in place sometime this afternoon. How about you?"

"I spoke to my supervisor about an hour ago. He said as long as I check in daily, he's got no problem with me working outside of the office. Besides, I'm providing more information than anyone else in our office."

Chapter 44

When Yousef awoke, he followed his new ritual of eating breakfast, going for a hike and planning his day. After his trek in the mountains, he wandered along Wyoming boulevard searching for a liquor store. Yousef had never been to a liquor store before, but to satisfy his plan, he needed to make a special purchase. He was looking for a large bottle of wine, and according to his strategy the wine needed to have been produced in New Mexico.

Strolling along the sidewalk, Yousef at last found the store that he had been in search of.

Quarters Discount Liquors was local Albuquerque retail liquor store known for its generous selection of wines and spirits. Entering the store, he looked at the well stocked selves displaying several varieties of beer, wine, and other alcoholic beverages. In particular, based on his earlier research, Yousef was looking for what was a 'magnum' sized bottle of a New Mexican white wine.

A salesclerk approached Yousef and asked if he could be of service. Yousef stated politely that he was looking for a magnum of wine to give as a gift. The clerk asked him how much he wanted to spend.

Yousef nervously replied, "I do not really know, how much does such a bottle cost?"

"Anywhere from around fifty dollars to several hundred," answered the salesclerk.

Yousef fingered the cash in his pocket. "Perhaps one hundred dollars," Yousef suggested.

The clerk pointed to a particular bottle, "this is a very fine, full bodied French wine," advised the salesperson.

"I'm actually looking for a local vintage," replied Yousef.

The clerk escorted Yousef further down the aisle, where he pulled a large bottle from the shelf. "This wine is produced right here in the south valley," informed the clerk.

Looking at the bottle, Yousef replied, "it looks like a red wine, but the gift is for my friend who enjoys white wine."

"Besides burgundy, this winemaker also produces this very fine chardonnay."

Looking at the large bottle, Yousef hesitated before responding, "I'll take it."

Taking the large bottle he walked to the check out line. When he placed the bottle on the counter, the clerk stated, "I'll need to see some ID."

Yousef panicked as salesclerk gazed firmly at him.

"No ID no sale," stated the clerk rigidly.

Yousef pulled his worn wallet from his jeans. He debated showing the clerk his drivers' license revealing his true identity. Finally resolute, Yousef handed the clerk his license. The clerk checked the date of his birth on his license.

"You're a lot older than you look," smiled the clerk.

"Yes," smiled Yousef, "I get that a lot."

Overcome with relief, he smiled to himself as he departed the store and walked back to his hideaway. He held onto the heavy wine bottle with both hands as he crossed the busy intersection at Tramway. Upon his return to his shed, he looked at the bottle with a calm appreciation. Then he hid his newly purchased treasure.

CHAPTER 45

TONY CLOSED HIS cell phone and mentioned to Sharon that the FBI was now monitoring the Imam's cell phone, his computer, and his hard wired telephone.

"It's hard to tell at this point if we'll stumble onto something, but at least we got our eye on the Imam," commented Tony.

"What exactly are you looking for Tony?"

"Well if the Imam talks to any other terrorism associates, either in the U.S. or overseas, will be able to monitor and record those discussions. Not only if he uses his phone, but also by way of his computer emails. We've subpoenaed his internet provider for previous records, but it might be a day or two before we receive them. In this case the Patriot Act is really helping us out," explained Tony.

"How is the Patriot Act different from any previous laws?" asked Sharon

"Good question. Under the old statue, the FBI was very limited on what records we were able to access. Emails, financial records, and telephone communications were very limited to what we could get, especially as it would apply to U.S. citizens. The Patriot Act also redefined 'terrorism' to include 'domestic terrorism.' This change in definition removes certain legal considerations between criminal investigations and surveillance. Under the old provisions we would not have access to the information we'll be able to get on the Imam. With the Patriot Act under U.S. Code Title 18, we can find out what the Imam views on his television and for how long."

"So," Sharon laughed, "We'll find out if the watches porn?"

"Yep," said Tony, smiling.

Chapter 46

A well rested Yousef enjoyed his ample breakfast, and walked a mountain trail for almost two hours before he focused his attention on his special undertaking. He held the previous day's purchase; the magnum of wine like it was a precious antiquity. He fingered the smooth glass and eyed the cork stopper. Finally he secreted the bottle next to his other hidden treasures and journeyed out toward the city.

Grinning to himself, he wandered into a neighborhood drug store. As he wandered the aisles, Yousef solemnly evaluated the varied articles on display. Stopping occasionally to pick up an item, he would scrutinize it, before carefully putting the merchandize back on the shelf. This activity consumed the better part of an hour. At last he selected three products that met with his inspection; a bees wax candle, a corkscrew, and a bubble wrapped package containing two nine volt batteries. He paid for his merchandise and walked out of the store.

Returning to his shed, Yousef methodically placed his recently purchased products onto his bed. Then he recovered the wine bottle from its hiding place. Sitting on his bed, he pondered how he should proceed with his current undertaking. He carefully examined the foil wrapping that covered the neck of the wine bottle and partially obscured the cork stopper. Picking up a razor knife, he cautiously cut the wrapping. Starting from the bottom he sliced the wrapping upward and across the top and then down through the opposite side. He gently removed the dark-green foil in two halves, mindful to retain the foil's molded shape.

He then pulled the stainless steel corkscrew from the plastic bag and looked attentively at the cork stopper. He lined up the business end of the corkscrew into the center of the cork, and slowly maneuvered the corkscrew into the stopper. When he was certain that the corkscrew was well into the stopper, he lowered the leveraging end of corkscrew onto the crown lip of the bottle. He took a deep breath, and then proceeded to extract the cork stopper. He slowly removed the stopper from the corkscrew and carefully put it aside.

CHAPTER 47

SA GARZA WENT to the Albuquerque Field Office to retrieve a fax. Sharon Martinez was on the phone with her office in Santa Fe. One of Sharon's work partners was able to provide some additional information on Imam Saadi. Tony returned to the townhouse as Sharon hung up the phone.

"Tony, I just got off the phone with one of my DHS colleagues. Seems our Imam has made several recent financial deposits into an account with Sunwest Bank," said Sharon.

"How much was deposited," asked Tony.

Referring to her notes Sharon replied, "During the last month three deposits were made of 25 thousand, one deposit of 35, and last week a deposit of 30 thousand dollars."

"Interesting," mumbled Tony.

"What did you find out?" asked Sharon.

Tony opened a manila envelop containing faxes he picked up at his office. "This is the Imam's phone records for the last six weeks. This is the result of yesterdays subpoena to his phone company. I've reviewed it briefly, and nothing in particular jumps out at me. Calls incoming and outgoing from mostly locals, with middle-eastern surnames," mentioned Tony.

"Could they be members of his mosque?" inquired Sharon

"Don't know Shar, but perhaps we should check."

"If I can get access to a classified computer Tony, I can run an ID check on all the names on your list."

"Okay Sharon, let's go get some lunch and then we stop back at my office."

"Just one condition," mentioned Sharon.

"What's that?"

"No more diners for me, at least till my stomach returns to its normal size," joked Sharon.

"Okay," laughed Tony.

CHAPTER 48

YOUSEF TOOK THE wine bottle outside of his shed and emptied the expensive wine onto the ground. He then carried the bottle back into the shed and attentively laid it upon his bed. Next, he picked up the cork stopper and working carefully with his razor knife, cut into the top center of the stopper. Slowly he cut away small chunks of cork. When he finished, the cork stopper had a pencil sized gap extending down lengthwise through the middle of the cork.

Now Yousef extracted one of stolen detonators from its hiding place. He carefully inserted the detonator into the stopper gauging the diameter of the detonator with the newly crafted opening in the cork. After making minor adjustments, Yousef was satisfied with the dry fit. He now picked up the concealed bag containing the nitro-methane fuel oil and set it on the ground outside of his shed. He then went back into shed and retrieved the empty wine bottle. Placing the wine bottle next the bag containing the fuel oil, he once again entered the shed.

Now he picked the cork stopper, the detonator, in addition to the beeswax candle. He walked outside of the shed and laid his items onto the iron table where he had earlier eaten breakfast. He repositioned the detonator into the stopper. The detonator's aluminum body was obscured inside the stopper with only the leg wires visible, extending from the top. He ignited the candle and gently dripped wax onto the cork stopper. This secured the detonator while further masking its presence.

Carefully setting the stopper/detonator onto the table, Yousef returned to the wine bottle. He opened two-liter plastic container and poured the fuel oil into the wine bottle. When filled, he retrieved the stopper and carefully reinserted the cork into the wine bottle. After reattaching the green colored foil, Yousef's task was almost complete.

The wine bottle looked the same as when it had been purchased with the exception of the wires extending from the top. He ensured that the wires were still shunted, and hid the explosive device behind an old wooden table inside the shed.

CHAPTER 49

PLUGGING IN THE names to the Department of Homeland Security 'watch list,' Sharon got three hits. Sharon explained to Tony how the list was developed.

"Under Homeland Security Presidential Directive (HSPD) 6, the Terrorist Screening Center (TSC) now provides 'one-stop shopping' so that every government screener is using the same terrorist watch list—whether it is an airport screener, an embassy official issuing visas overseas, or a state or local law enforcement officer on the street. The TSC allows government agencies to run name checks against the same comprehensive list with the most accurate, up-to-date information about known and suspected terrorists," Sharon clarified.

"So what does the 'hit' on these names actually mean?"

"The only thing that I can say for certain is that these men were placed on the watch list for some suspicious activity. These could be nontraditional financial transactions, unusual travel plans, or associations with suspect groups."

"So being on the list, does not necessarily rule in-or-out their being bad actors?"

"Right Tony, it just gives us a starting point to connect the dots."

"I would suggest we contact these individuals and see what connection they might provide with the Imam."

Tony copied the three individual's names, current listed address, and telephone information.

Sharon and Tony decided to start with the closest listed address first, working toward the middle of the city.

"Gee Tony," Sharon commented, as they got into Tony's government vehicle, "this field work takes a lot of energy."

"You got that right."

CHAPTER 50

AFTER PAINSTAKINGLY WORKING on his "bomb," Yousef decided to take a break. He put on his red hat an ambled toward the library. One important portion of the bombs' design still eluded him. As he wandered in the general direction of the public library, he focused profoundly on this predicament. He needed a concealed switch that connected the battery with the detonator. He decided to research available options on the internet.

When he arrived at the library, the computer carrel that he had used for the last few days was occupied so he selected another computer cubicle located closer to the librarian's desk. He searched for "improvised switches," and visited dozens of websites. After several hours, with a determined intensity he came upon simple method that he was satisfied would work with his explosive device. Before he left the library he searched the internet for the closest retail store in which to purchase his newly required items.

Yousef walked to the *Michaels Arts and Crafts* outlet on Wyoming boulevard. Again, as was his nature, he slowly perused each aisle scanning every self. Spending nearly an hour in the store, he finally selected his objects of interest. He purchased a packet of metal thumbtacks, a container of miniature plastic clothespins, a tube of rubber cement, and a large red fabric bow. Walking back to his hideaway, he contemplated his plan.

When he arrived at his shed, he arranged the newly purchased articles on his bed. Opening the container of clothespins, Yousef selected one, and tested its function. Next he pulled two thumbtacks from their packet. Very meticulously, he pushed each thumbtack into the internal and opposite sides on the clamping end of the small clothespin. He depressed the clothespin repeatedly after this assembly, ensuring that, in the closed position. the metal tacks made contact with each other. Next he placed a small square of rubber inner-tube, between the two contact points.

Finally, Yousef was ready to complete his bomb. He carefully pulled out the wine bottle from behind the table. Sitting on his bed and securing the bottle between his legs, he carefully separated the detonator's leg wires from their shunt. He cut one leg wire in half keeping the 101 millimeter severed piece. From this piece, he cut off 25 millimeters of the plastic insulation, cautious of not severing the cooper wire. He now wrapped the loose cooper wire around a tack imbedded in the clothespin. With the other short wire still connected to the detonator, he mated the remaining wire with the opposite thumbtack. Making sure the rubber square was securely back in place, he now connected the unfastened end of wire to the positive post of the 9 volt battery. The remaining, long leg wire coming from the detonator, he attached to the negative post of the battery.

Yousef's bomb was now operational. To function, all he needed to do was to pull out the rubber insulation from between the tacks which completed the circuit, initiating the blasting cap, and detonation of the fuel oil.

He now glued the battery lengthwise onto the top of the bottle leaving enough room to secure the miniature plastic clothespin. Looking over his work, he fastened the large red bow onto the battery which effectively concealed the battery along with the makeshift switch.

Breathing heavily, he returned the completed bomb to its hiding place.

After concealing his bomb, he wandered around the deserted backyard deeply in thought. After several minutes he returned to the shed and lay down to rest. Moments later he was sound asleep.

Chapter 51

When Tony and Sharon arrived at the first address on Sharon's watch list, Tony knocked repeatedly but no one answered. They decided to move on to the second name on the list.

The address listed was approximately two miles away from the mosque, in a quiet non-descript neighborhood in southeast Albuquerque. Tony, with Sharon following to his rear approached the residence and Tony knocked on the front door. They could hear movement inside the home. Moments later the front door opened slightly.

"Yes?" a woman's voice inquired.

Tony could barely make out the individual in the darkened vestibule. "I'm Special Agent Garza with the FBI, and this Sharon Martinez with the Department of Homeland Security. We would like a moment of your time to ask you a few questions."

"My husband is not home," the woman responded softly.

"Please ma'am, this will take just a couple minutes of your time."

With that, the door opened to reveal a petite Muslim woman with a small female child clutching at her leg. The woman was wearing a brown hijab that covered her from head to neck. She wore a loose fitting off-white burqa that enveloped her body down to her ankles. The small child was dressed in brightly flowered dress. "Come," said the woman, opening the door further.

Tony and Sharon followed the woman and child into a small living space. Sparsely furnished with a white patterned sofa, green pastel side chairs, and large brass floor lamp, the room was small but appeared clean and uncluttered. The woman gestured to the sofa, "Please have seat."

Tony and Sharon took a seat on the sofa as the woman asked, "Can I get you some tea?"

Sharon responded, "That would be wonderful."

The woman retreated from the room along with the child, still clutching at her leg. Moments later the women returned with diminutive brass cups and a brass urn. She poured a steaming milky green liquid from the urn into each of the cups. She served Tony the first cup, and offered the remaining cup to Sharon.

Taking a sip, Sharon declared, "This is very good."

"Its Arabian tea," replied the woman.

To put the woman at ease, Tony offered, "Your daughter is very lovely."

"Thank you, her name is Afrah and its meaning is 'happiness.'"

"Have you lived in the United States long?" asked Tony.

"We arrived here just over one year ago, when my husband was offered a temporary position at the university," volunteered the woman.

Sharon noticed that the women spoke with a strong British accent and presented a very formal—almost regal demeanor.

Tony continued asking questions politely. "Do you and your husband have many friends in the area?"

"Not as many acquaintances as we've had back home. Sometimes some of my husband's work associates drop by for dinner, and once or twice their families have stopped by for a brief visit. However, it is not like living back home where my mother and sisters would visit most everyday."

"Are you homesick?" asked Sharon.

"Oh very much," replied the woman.

CHAPTER 52

WITH HIS WEAPON completed, Yousef had yet to formulate his plan for an appropriate target. He was confident Allah would reveal the intended victim in due time. When he rose from his bed, he found the property's proprietor setting out the morning meal.

"Yousef," the owner said, "How was your sleep?"

"Very pleasant," replied Yousef.

"What are your plans today?"

"After enjoying this great meal, I plan to hike in the mountains. Then I'll go to the library and do research," responded Yousef.

"Assalaam Alaikum, Yousef."

"Wa Alaikum assalaam," rejoined Yousef.

Yousef hiked throughout the morning letting his mind wander while enjoying the brilliant sunlight, rugged terrain, and oneness with nature. In the early afternoon he ambled again toward the public library.

In the library, he sat at his favored computer terminal reading current media reports and commentary. Eventually, he came upon news article that caused Yousef to ponder. The article was from the *Washington Post*. The editorial detailed the "United States War on Terror," and mentioned that the U.S. President along with his newly appointed Secretary of the Department Homeland Secretary, were planning a rapid tour of western states that were the most recent victims of the terrorist mayhem. The story concluded that after the president's whirlwind visit to the western states, the president planned to conclude his trip with a stop at the site of the Twin Towers devastation in New York City. It was suggested that the president intended to deliver a speech in honor of the many men and women who had lost their lives, and to commemorate the "9/11" one year anniversary.

"Insha'Allah," whispered Yousef to himself.

CHAPTER 53

SPENDING THE BETTER part of an hour with the Muslim woman, Tony and Sharon left with little more information than when they arrived. However, clarifying facts had started to emerge. The woman confirmed that her husband infrequently attended Imam Saadi's mosque. She said her husband was a visiting professor at the University of New Mexico (engineering department), and had professional associations with colleagues throughout the Middle East. These associates, the woman maintained, included Muslims in Pakistan, Saudi Arabia, and Palestine. The women claimed to be unaware of the specifics of her husband's dealings with these men.

"Let's hit the next address," suggested Tony. "Can you read off the address for me?"

"Sure," after giving Tony the address, Sharon asked where it was at.

"Glenwood Hills," said Tony. "It's a pretty nice neighborhood, in the Sandia foothills right off of Tramway."

Twenty-five minutes later, Tony and Sharon proceeded as before, knocking and ringing the door bell. "Looks like nobody home," pronounced Tony.

"What say we knockoff for a few hours Sharon. Maybe try again after dark."

"Okay Tony."

"Well go back to my place. I'll fix us some dinner. Then we'll try these two addresses again."

"Sounds good, Tony. I wish this was easier. But I guess we just have to gut it out."

"Nobody ever suggested that law enforcement was easy, Sharon."

Chapter 54

By scouring the internet, with any tidbits of information that he could glean on the President's travel schedule, Yousef was able to reasonably deduce some information. Working backwards, he knew that the President was planning on giving a commemoration speech in New York at two o'clock on the afternoon of September 11th, which was two days away. Various news stories reported that the President along with various U.S. governmental dignitaries, planned on making short visits to California, Nevada, Arizona, Texas, and New Mexico. Based on previous tours by the President, Yousef expected the President's itinerary to visit two or three states per day. If he started with the most Western states, like California, Arizona, and Nevada, he theorized that the travel planners would save Texas and New Mexico for early on the last day, prior to moving on for his afternoon speech in New York. So, he calculated, he would have one day to determine where and when the President would be arriving and delivering his address in New Mexico.

He was also able to learn, based the President's previous state visits, that the state's governor would often times welcome the President to his or her state. Finally, he determined that the only public airport in New Mexico which *Air Force One* was able to land at was the Albuquerque Sunport.

Yousef walked back to his hideaway feeling quite relaxed. He was once again about to execute his mission, however this time he felt tranquil and at peace with himself. "Allah will help me," Yousef resolved.

When he entered his shed; he pulled out his explosive bottle and fingered it fondly. He gently returned the bottle to its previous concealed location. Once more he lay down on his bed, and was soon fast asleep.

CHAPTER 55

SHARON AND TONY returned to Tony's townhouse. Tony was outside on his patio, barbequing a flank steak while Sharon, inside, was preparing roasted onions, peppers, and a local favorite, *Moriarty* sweet corn. Normally, Tony would be enjoying a Corona while making his dinner, but as he explained to Sharon, "I don't drink when I have to go back to work."

Enjoying their dinner together, Tony stood up and began clearing their dinner plates from the kitchen table. After a quick trip to the bathroom, Sharon helped Tony to finish cleaning up from their meal. Shortly after 06:00 P.M., Tony and Sharon were traveling to Rio Rancho with the hope that this time the individual in question would be at home. Arriving at the residence about twenty minutes later, Tony approached the front door with Sharon trailing behind him. Knocking and waiting several times, a somewhat discouraged Tony stated, "well looks like he's not at home. I suggest we move on to the Glenwood Hills address and save this one for a return visit tomorrow."

Travel to the northeast Albuquerque address was slow due to heavy traffic. "I think the New Mexican State Fair is in town, Tony."

"Well its really screwed up traffic in this area," remarked Tony.

Minutes later they arrived at the Glenwood Hills address. "Well the lights are on Sharon, maybe we'll be luckier with this one."

Tony rang the door bell, and a few moments later a medium sized male opened the door. The man had thick, black hair going gray. He had a well groomed beard, and had reading glasses dangling by a cord around his neck. "Yes?" inquired the man.

Tony introduced himself and Sharon, and told the man that he would like to ask him some questions related to Imam Saadi and his mosque. "Sure," said the man, gesturing Tony and Sharon to have a seat in one of the wrought-iron chairs situated on the front porch. After Tony and Sharon were seated, the man asked, "So how can I be of help to you Special Agent Garza?"

"Well sir, we are presently involved with an investigation involving the recent terrorist activities," replied Tony.

"How does this relate to Imam Saadi?" inquired the man.

"Well," said Tony, "are you aware the alleged suspects were members of the Imam's mosque?"

Visually disturbed, the man nervously replied, "Well no, not really."

"What does 'not really' mean?"

"I do not know all of the people who worship at the mosque," the man replied in a wavering voice.

"What is your relationship with the Imam?"

"He is my Imam, and we have been acquainted for several years," the man sputtered.

"Besides using the mosque as your place of worship, what other associations do you have with the Imam?" Tony probed.

"I donate money to the mosque," the man volunteered.

"How much money?" asked Tony.

"I think our discussions are over!" the man shouted, entering his home and slamming the front door, leaving Tony and Sharon alone on the porch.

Getting back into their car, Tony opined, "Me thinks this man is overly sensitive."

CHAPTER 56

YOUSEF AWOKE WELL rested before sunrise. When he peered out from the shed he saw the owner seated at the iron table and talking animatedly on a cell phone. Joining the man at the table, he waited until his host had finished his call before greeting him.

"Sabah al khair (good morning)," Yousef declared.

The man did not reply, and appeared anxious. Finally the man stood and said, "Maasalaamah, Yousef (Goodbye)."

The man stumbled into his house, clearly upset. Yousef did not understand what was troubling his kind host, but he decided to eat his breakfast and continue with his tasks for the day.

After his meal he walked briskly into town in search of another item to fulfill his impending mission. On Lomas boulevard, Yousef wandered into a *Target* retail store. As usual, he took his time meandering throughout the store. Finally he purchased a black backpack and hiked back to the public library.

Exploring the internet was a means for Yousef to easily obtain information, and allowed him to perfect his mission. He was able to access phone numbers of the New Mexican governor's office. Once he written down specific numbers, he made the bold move of phoning the governor's personal administrative assistant.

Using a public pay phone, Yousef called the governor's secretary. "This is Juan from Albuquerque Sunport security office," Yousef stated, while trying to act authoritative.

"Yes," intoned a friendly female voice.

"I want to re-verify the governor's schedule relative to the VIP visit tomorrow," uttered Yousef.

"We've been over this several times now," stated the secretary. "What can I tell you?"

"As a matter of security," Yousef pleaded, "I just want to make sure we have everything covered."

"Well I guess I can appreciate that," recited the secretary. "Once again, the governor plans on arriving at 8:00 A.M. sharp. The VIP's plane lands at 8:30, short speech by VIP followed by a meet and greet for no more than 30 minutes at the airport tarmac, and we expect wheels up at 9:30."

"Got it," sighed, Yousef, "I did not mean to bother you. We just wanted to ensure that our schedules were on track."

"No bother," said the secretary as she hung up the phone.

"Insha'Allah," Yousef whispered to himself as he walked back to his hideaway.

CHAPTER 57

TONY RECEIVED A phone call from his field office at 5:17 A.M. "Sorry to wake you so early in the morning Tony. But we just received a translation from a voice recording on Imam Saadi's phone. The call was recorded late last evening and we sent it to headquarters for translation. We received the transcripts about twenty minutes ago. You need to come in and read it."

"I'll be there in fifteen," said Tony as he hung up the phone.

Tony was dressed in less than five minutes. As he retrieved his keys, he knocked on Sharon's bedroom door. "Yes," responded Sharon in a sleep induced voice.

"Sharon, I've got to run over to my office. I'll fill you in later. Bye."

As Tony rushed into the field office, a member of the Joint Terrorism Task Force or better known as the JTTF greeted Tony. "Hey Tony, sorry to screw with your beauty sleep, but this might be hot."

"Not a problem," muttered Tony as he took the stack of transcripts.

Tony retreated to his desk as he methodically reviewed the records. Ten minutes later Tony looked up from his desk and smiled at his colleague.

"Not a whole lot here, but maybe enough. I interviewed this guy last night and after a couple of questions, he clammed up, looks like when I left, he phoned the Imam."

"What's interesting," stated Tony, "is that this guy was anxious when we showed up, but got really nervous when I questioned him about his association with the Imam. When I asked him about monetary donations, that's when he stopped talking."

Looking at the transcripts, Tony pointed to a passage, "And here he refers to 'money transfers.' Also, it's somewhat lost in the translation, but he's asking what he should do about 'federal agents' and then the Imam tells him to 'settle down' and 'they don't know anything.' What's particularly interesting is at the end of the call, the Imam asks him how 'our little leader is doing.'"

"We need a search warrant now!" commanded Tony, "Looks like he might be harboring a fugitive at his residence."

CHAPTER 58

YOUSEF WOKE FROM a restful slumber and peered from the shed. He saw his host more relaxed and reading a newspaper at the iron table. Yousef bid him 'good morning,' and sat across from the man at the table.

"Eat up, Yousef!" said the man, "You need your strength." As Yousef ate, the man questioned him regarding his schedule for the day.

"My mission is nearing completion," said Yousef. "I plan to travel to the airport this morning, and Insha'Allah, my destiny will be achieved."

"Insha'Allah," repeated the man.

The man retreated into his home, as Yousef prepared for his day. Yousef carefully put the improvised wine bottle into his recently purchased backpack. Putting on the backpack, he then wheeled out the bicycle and carefully inspected the chain, tires, and gears. Then he walked the bike down to the street, jumped aboard and peddled down the mountain road.

A few blocks before the airport, he got off of the bicycle and abandoned it behind a derelict warehouse. Feeling confident, he strolled to the entrance of the Albuquerque airport. Once inside, he noticed several security personnel. He calmly approached a uniformed guard, and asked, "When is the governor arriving?"

"Why do you want to know, little man?"

"I'm supposed to meet with the governor, as I have a special present for the special guests to our state," responded Yousef.

"What present?" inquired the guard.

Yousef took off his backpack, unzipped the flap, and pulled the wine bottle from the pack. "I'm presenting, along with the governor, this special bottle of New Mexican wine for our special guests."

"Okay," said the guard, "follow me."

The guard walked Yousef out of the airport terminal to a chain-link fence, on the eastern side of the tarmac. Many security personnel were clustered around the tarmac. The guard strolled up to another security individual and called out, "Hey Phil, this little man says he supposed to meet with the governor to present a bottle of wine to the POTUS."

"First I've heard of it, but the governor's entourage is 'bout five minutes out. Just stand here for the time being. They should be pulling up right over there."

CHAPTER 59

"SHARON WE'RE PREPARING a search warrant for the engineer we interviewed last evening. If you're ready to roll in five minutes, I'll pick you up on our way back to Glenwood Hills?"

"I'm ready and waiting," replied Sharon, hanging up the phone.

In less than sixty minutes, three black, FBI Chevy Suburban's pulled in front of the Glenwood Hills residence. Tony asked that the other FBI agents to stay back while he approached the home. Knocking on the front door, Tony yelled, "FBI, open up."

Tony noticed movement at a front window. A dark figure was looking out toward the street. Again, Tony shouted, "FBI, open up."

Slowly the front door opened to reveal the visibly shaken owner.

"I have search warrant," commanded Tony.

"Now tell me where is Yousef Khan?"

"Who?" muttered the owner.

"I'm not playing around, Sir. Tell me now where Yousef Khan is!" shouted Tony.

The man paled and sat on the front steps. "I'm not sure where he is, he mentioned earlier he was going to the airport."

"What's he doing at the airport?" asked Tony.

"Honestly, I do not know," murmured the man.

Tony walked over to one of his FBI partners and told him to search the home and then 'book' the dazed owner. He then instructed his colleagues to follow him to the airport, in pursuit of Yousef Khan.

Chapter 60

Yousef waited patiently while Governor Richards' chauffeured car drove slowly onto the tarmac. As the governor was helped from the vehicle, the guard named 'Phil' wandered up to the governor and mentioned, "Governor, your little friend is waiting for you."

"What friend?" asked the Governor.

"The little man over there," pointed the guard.

Governor Richards approached Yousef. "Who are you?"

"I'm Juan Valdez," explained Yousef, "I'm a student at the university and I've bought this New Mexican bottle of wine to give to the President."

"Very good Juan," said Governor Richards, "just stay by me, and at the appropriate time we'll make the presentation.

Juan politely smiled, as he fingered the rubber tab on the top of the bottle.

The governor wandered around making small talk and shaking hands with local media personalities, the Kirtland Air Force Base commander, the Albuquerque mayor, and other dignitaries.

Yousef grinned to himself as he visualized how his plan was unfolding. The airport security guard, the New Mexican Governor, and soon, the President of the United States, would all be taken in by his brilliant deception. Stoically shadowing the Governor, nobody seemed aware of his presence. He followed the Governor through the crowd of onlookers silently awaiting the President's arrival. As he reflected on his invisibility, he considered that in a very short time they all would be aware of his presence.

CHAPTER 61

"**WHAT HAPPENED?**" **ASKED** Sharon, as Tony hurried back into the driver's seat.

"We're off to the airport," replied Tony. "I'll explain on the way."

Tony turned on the vehicle's emergency lights as he sped away from the residence. "Seems this guy has been hiding Yousef Khan," reported Tony. "He tells us Khan left for the airport early this morning."

"Is he catching a flight?" asked Sharon.

"Claims he doesn't know."

"Hey Tony," responded Sharon, "while you were at your office, I heard on the radio that some VIP's were landing at the airport sometime this morning."

"Who?" asked Tony.

"Although, they would not say for sure, there was some speculation that the VIP's might include the President of the United States."

"Shit," Tony muttered and stomped on the gas.

Tony pulled into airport terminal not knowing exactly where to go. He ran into the ticket area where he flagged down a security guard. "I'm Special Agent Garza, and I need to speak with your supervisor immediately."

"Not going to happen," the guard replied, "All our brass are out on the tarmac awaiting the VIP's arrival."

"Specifically," Tony asked, "what VIP's?"

"Well," responded the guard, "starting with the President, the Secretary of Homeland Security, the governor, the mayor, and that's all that I currently know about."

"Shit," said Tony, "we have reason to believe, that a Middle Eastern terrorist might be here at the airport. Can you get me out to the tarmac?"

The guard pulled out his radio and mumbled something unintelligible. Spoke some more, then told Tony to follow.

"Who is she?" asked the guard, as Sharon walked up beside Tony.

"She's with me."

CHAPTER 62

JUAN STAYED AT Governor Richards' side as *Air Force One* taxied next to the tarmac. When the plane was parked and chocked, a portable stairway was hauled over to the main passenger doorway. The doorway opened and moments later the Secretary of Homeland Security emerged waving to the small crowd as he descended the stairs. Seconds later, the President of the United States was visible in the doorway speaking to an aide. Smiling, the President waved to the crowd of onlookers as he moved down the stairway. The Secretary, waited for the President at the bottom of the flight of steps. When the President arrived, the Secretary moved to his rear, and whispered something into his ear.

Governor Richards looked down toward Juan, "Juan, stay here and I'll introduce you to the President as soon as he finishes his speech."

Richards then was led over to the President where they shook hands and exchanged greetings. Moving toward a raised podium on the left side of the tarmac, the President, the Secretary of Homeland Security, followed by the Governor, took their assigned positions on the elevated platform.

"People of the great state of New Mexico

Our great nation continues to be tested in a way that we have not been since the start of the Cold War. We saw what a handful of our enemies can do with box-cutters and plane tickets. We see them blemishing our landscape with rode flares. We hear their threats to launch even more terrible attacks on our people. And we know that if they were able to get their hands on weapons of mass destruction, they would use them against us. We face an enemy determined to bring death and suffering into our homes. America did not ask for this war, and every American wishes it were over. So do I. But the war is not over -- and it will not be over until either we or the extremists emerge victorious. If we do not defeat these enemies now, we will leave our children to face a Middle East overrun by terrorist states and radical dictators armed with nuclear weapons. We are in a war that will set the course for this new century -- and determine the destiny of millions across the world. As you know, last week I ordered for the dismantlement of our entire nuclear stockpile. It is my sincere hope that all nations, large or small, follow our example as a gesture of lasting peace.

I also would like to honor those who toil day and night to keep our homeland safe, and we are giving them the tools they need to protect our people. We've created the Department of Homeland Security. We have torn down the wall that kept law enforcement and intelligence from sharing information. We've tightened security at our airports and seaports and borders, and we've created new programs to monitor enemy bank records and phone calls. Thanks to the hard work of our law enforcement and intelligence professionals, we have broken up terrorist cells in our midst and saved American lives.

Dangerous enemies have declared their intention to destroy our way of life. They're not the first to try, and their fate will be the same as those who tried before. Nine-Eleven showed us why. The attacks were meant to bring us to our knees, and they did, but not in the way the terrorists intended. Americans with unflinching resolve grew steadfast that our enemies would not have the last word. The spirit of our people is the source of America's strength. And we go forward with trust in that spirit, confidence in our purpose, and faith in a loving God who made us to be free.

Gracias y que Dios los bendiga. (*Thank you, and may God bless you*)."

Chapter 63

As the President of the United States was giving his speech, Tony with the aid of the Sunport security personnel, scanned the assembled crowd. Nothing appeared out of the ordinary. Tony methodically walked throughout the area, paying particular attention to small, Middle Eastern looking, males. With Sharon at his side, Special Agent Garza watched the assembled spectators.

When the President finished, the crowd politely clapped and cheered in approval of the President's remarks. Governor Richards conversed shortly with the President before leading him toward the onlookers. Yousef stood fast, anticipating the precise moment to engage his target.

"Mr. President, I would like you to meet my good friend Juan," the animated Governor explained, "Juan has a special New Mexican gift for you."

Walking briskly toward the young man, the President stopped abruptly about six feet from where Juan was waiting patiently. He pulled a handkerchief from a rear pocket and coughed into it. Not anticipating the President's action, the Governor was already facing Juan, and had placed his thick arm across Juan's left shoulder, meant as a gesture of endearment. Realizing suddenly that the President was three paces to his rear, the New Mexican Governor turned quickly to reengage the President.

When the Governor made this vigorous move, Juan who was clutching the wine bottle rigidly, stumbled to his right and the bottle fell from his firm grasp. As the bottle crashed against the hard, blacktop surface, the glass shattered into dozens of tiny fragments, splashing clear liquid onto the tarmac.

Juan recovered from his fall, but as he stood up, tears were bubbling from his eyes. "I'm so sorry Juan," the sympathetic Governor moaned.

The President moved forward and grasped Juan's trembling hand. "That's okay young man, I certainly appreciate your kind gesture."

The Governor continued leading the President through the crowd, shaking hands and making small talk.

A despondent Juan wandered slowly from the tarmac.

CHAPTER 64

SHARON AND TONY continued to examine faces and body language just outside the throng of exuberant citizens. A short time later the President, followed by the Secretary of Homeland Security were escorted onto the waiting aircraft. As the crowd began to disperse, Sharon found herself standing in the middle of the broken glass shards and puddly liquid.

"Tony, come look at this," whispered Sharon. She pointed downward at the remaining neck of the broken wine bottle.

Looking to where Sharon was indicating, Tony nodded. He then walked promptly over to the security supervisor and said, "Get all of these people out of here now! We have a bomb."

The Albuquerque Bomb Squad was on scene within the hour. Police forensics examiners collected the rendered-safe detonator, large pieces of the broken bottle, swabs of the liquid, and the remaining red bow. Tony was on the phone giving his field office a blow-by-blow report.

Governor Richards was in route back to Santa Fe, unaware of the activity since his departure. Tony was able to obtain the Governor's private cell phone number and dialed several times before getting a connection. "Governor this is Special Agent

Garza with the FBI. After the President's plane took off and you left the area we found remnants of a bomb on the tarmac."

"Jesucristo!" exclaimed the Governor.

"Sir, I need you to calm down. We have the bomb components safely contained. Now I need to ask you some questions concerning the alleged perpetrator."

"How would I know the perpetrator?" the Governor shouted into his cell phone.

"Sir, who was the young Hispanic man that you were with on the tarmac, the one wearing the red ball cap?" inquired Tony.

"How should I know, I just met him as I arrived? He said his name was Juan and he had a bottle of wine for the President," muttered the Governor.

"Well sir, that was not a bottle of wine, it was an improvised bomb."

"¡Mierda!" exclaimed the Governor.

CHAPTER 65

A CRESTFALLEN YOUSEF wandered listlessly from the airport. As he drifted onto Gibson boulevard, he moved toward the derelict building where he had abandoned his bicycle just hours before. He squatted next to the mountain bike and sobbed silently. Eventually, he summoned enough strength to get on the bicycle and drove aimlessly toward the Sandia Mountains.

Eventually he found himself on Tramway boulevard heading north. Instinctively, without focus, he neared the neighborhood where he had resided for the last few days. Coming upon the engineer's home on the right, he noticed several police vehicles and yellow 'crime scene tape' draped around the owner's residence. Yousef stopped suddenly comprehending the activity. He then quickly turned the bike around and peddled back onto Tramway.

Twenty minutes later, he found himself at the foot of Sandia Peak Tram. He scrutinized a sign pointing to the La Luz Trail. Yousef mechanically discarded the bike, and slogged onto a mountain path.

Mindlessly he plotted upward higher and higher. As the afternoon wore on, the sky became dark and overcast. Gentle breezes turned into harsh winds and the fair temperature evolved into a biting chill.   He continued upward wandering unconsciously.

Around nightfall, engulfed in darkness, Yousef stumbled and fell hard against an unforgiving granite boulder. He tried to stand but was overcome with fatigue, mutually borne to his mind and body. At last surrendering, he collapsed into a fetal position. With his knees to his chest, he cried himself to sleep.

Chapter 66

When all the evidence was bagged and transported from airport, Tony and Sharon drove back to the engineer's home at the Glenwood Hills address. Local Albuquerque Police along with FBI investigators had sealed off the home, and were still busy combing over the owner's extensive personal possessions and storage niches.

Tony flashed his badge in the direction of APD patrolman as he and Sharon ducked under the yellow barrier tape. As they entered the home, Tony's FBI colleague met them at the foyer.

"Hey Tony, I heard you had a little excitement at the airport."

Tony grimaced, "Yea, we should have had our perp—we were looking right at him, but didn't realize it. Then he just walked away. He's probably real spooked right now. But we'll get him. Find anything here?"

"This place is massive. We've bagged all the papers from his office, tried to access his computer, but couldn't break his password. So we're going to take the whole shebang in and let our computer folks crack it."

"So you're almost done here?" inquired Tony.

"We still have the garage to go through, along with a storage shed out back, probably another couple of hours at least," provided the agent.

"I'll stay out of your way. It looks like you got everything under control," Tony replied, escorting Sharon back to the front veranda.

Taking a seat at an iron table on the front porch, Sharon asked, "What now Tony?"

"We wait."

CHAPTER 67

FORTY-FIVE MINUTES LATER Tony and Sharon could hear a loud verbal exchanges coming from the back yard of the Glenwood Hills home. Sharon followed Tony around the side of the house into the back yard. An energetic forensics investigator, wearing nylon gloves and paper booties, was holding up an object. "Look what I found," smiled the investigator. "I've got a blasting cap, and a partial bottle of nitro. It also looks like someone was sleeping back here. There are clean sheets and blankets covering an old mattress. Also I've got, what looks to be, a brand new tee-shirt."

Tony walked over to the investigator. "Good work. We need to run the serial number on that cap ASAP," suggested Tony.

"I'll do it as soon as I return to the station," beamed the investigator.

Tony ambled over to the shed and peered inside. Deep in thought, he stood silently and assessed the tight surroundings. Sharon quietly walked up beside Tony. She did not want to disturb him, however she was trying to understand what was running through his mind. At last she spoke up.

"Well what do you think Tony?"

"I'm just trying to imagine, what makes this guy tick. Living in a shed—building bombs, it just doesn't make sense to me."

"There is one thing we do know Tony."

"What's that?"

"Well, we do know it makes sense to Yousef Khan, irrational or not," offered Sharon.

Tony walked over to his FBI partner. "I'm out of here; we are going over to the lockup facility to reengage the engineer."

Tony and Sharon drove over to detention facility in northwest Albuquerque. "So what do you think about law enforcement work Sharon?" asked Tony.

"Well it bothers me that we had the kid in our sights, and he got away."

"We'll get him yet. Were just lucky he hasn't hurt anybody," said Tony.

"At least, not yet," mumbled Sharon.

Chapter 68

WAKING UP EARLY the next morning Tony sat at his kitchen table and reviewed his notes from the previous day. The late night interview with the Sandia engineer proved helpful.

When Tony asked the engineer how he had befriended the fugitive Yousef Khan, the engineer told him that he did not know Khan, but was asked by the Imam to provide him some shelter. The engineer agreed, claiming that he did not realize that Khan was wanted by the authorities. As for the money transfers, the engineer claimed he had organized a group of Pakistani friends which sought out donations for displaced Muslims. He maintained that he collected the monies and then transferred the funds to the Imam. The engineer was concerned because he had a government "top secret" clearance and one of the requirements in preserving the clearance was to volunteer any association with foreign nationals. Since, some the donated money came from sources other than U.S. citizens, he was worried that he had violated his security agreement. He did not want to reveal this association, because it might target innocent people who were respectable and just wanted to help the displaced, poor Muslims.

When Tony pressed the engineer for more information on Khan, he was emphatic that he was not aware of Khan's activities. He said that he fed Khan, allowed him to sleep in his outside storage shelter, and had no other involvement with the young man. Further he stated that Khan was polite, but refused to discuss his activities other than to casually mention that he would hike in the mountains and make a visit to the local library. When asked how Khan traveled, the engineer said that the boy either walked or took his blue mountain bike.

Two hours later Sharon awoke and joined Tony at the kitchen table. "I don't know how you do it Tony?"

"Do what?

"Pull a fifteen hour shift and get up before dawn."

"That's what law enforcement and catching the bad guys is all about," said Tony grinning broadly.

Chapter 69

Yousef woke up disorientated, sleeping under a massive juniper tree. Still despondent from the previous day's chain of events, he sat upon a granite ledge and cried.

The sunny autumn day suddenly turned chilly and overcast. Gray cirrus clouds dominated the skyline. Before noon, a light drizzle turned into a heavy downpour. Yousef sat seemingly unfazed by the intense precipitation. The dreary atmosphere seemed in concert with his burgeoning depression. For hours on end he sat perched on a boulder, unable to move or concentrate.

Just before nightfall, a lobo appeared three meters to the right of Yousef. The gray wolf's piercing, gold-tinted eyes stayed frozen on Yousef's presence. The animal would adjust his front legs, tilt his head slightly, but the unblinking eyes stared vigilantly.

At last, Yousef finally detected the creature. Still confused Yousef was at first startled, then surrendered to his ultimate fate. He gazed back at the wolf and smirked. Both man and animal continued their watchful exchange throughout the evening.

Around midnight Yousef awoke from a reverie, realizing that the lobo was gone. Off in the distance, he heard a deafening howl. Yousef interpreted this as a sign.

He stood for the first time in over ten hours. Famished he rambled up a steep path looking for nourishment. He eventually came upon a large building. He circled the edifice. Nightlights were present on the building although it appeared to be vacant. Finally he noticed a sign indicating that the structure was called the *High Finance Restaurant.* He waited, and then furtively pried open a window and entered.

Once inside the restaurant, he crept along its darkened passageways making his way into the food preparation area. He noticed an outsized refrigerator, and pulled on the stainless steel handle. He spied an assortment of foodstuffs, and greedily stuffed himself with raw meat, lettuce, avocados, tomatoes, and black beans.

After Yousef satisfied his raging hunger, he quietly departed the restaurant climbing out through the opened window.

CHAPTER 70

AT 09:05 A.M., Special Agent Garza received a call from a regional ATF agent. The agent indicated that they had tracked the lot numbers of the two recovered detonators. Copying down the details, Tony hung up the phone.

"We're out of here Sharon."

"What have we got?" inquired Sharon as she accompanied Tony to the SUV.

"Roadrunner Mining and Construction Company, that's where the Khan obtained the detonators," Tony explained.

Within the hour Tony and Sharon were sitting in the cramped construction trailer just outside of Edgewood, New Mexico. Both the burley foreman and "Red" the demolition crew chief were enjoying their third cup of coffee of the day.

"I can't explain how someone would be able to get their hands on any of our explosives. Everything is under lock and key and we keep a log of all of our expenditures each day," mumbled Red.

Tony then laid a composite picture of Yousef Khan on the counter. "That looks like that Mexican kid from last week," suggested Red.

"What Mexican kid?" asked Tony.

"Well early last week the kid wandered in here. I think he said he was an engineering student at the university. Said he wanted to learn more about road construction and demolition for his degree or some shit. Seemed like a nice kid, polite and would help out with whatever we asked him," said the foreman.

"Did he get around any explosives?" inquired Tony.

"Yep," stated Red. "His last day here, he helped with the demo in the south valley. Worked hard too, seemed to pick up things real fast."

"Well he picked up a couple of your detonators, real fast," added Tony.

"Why would he do that?" muttered Red shaking his head.

"This kid is a Middle-Eastern terrorist," added Tony.

The foreman and Red stood dumbfounded as Tony and Sharon departed.

CHAPTER 71

YOUSEF SLEPT MOST of the daylight hours and foraged during the late evening and into the night. He discovered a shallow cave which he occupied during the day. He padded the hard limestone floor with pine straw and soft foliage. When he woke from his slumber just after sunset, he would climb the steep mountain paths and perch on rugged boulders, where he would gaze spellbound, into the valley below.

To a casual observer, Yousef Khan's unkempt appearance coupled with his rather bizarre behavior of staring into the distance for long periods of time would evoke complex discussions on human pathology. The etiology of this behavior would be cloaked in mystery, supposition, and psychological theory. A behaviorist might suggest that Yousef's actions have been "conditioned" to evoke his current reaction with the environment that he found himself ensnared.

Disregarding the previous day's misfortunes, Yousef mind and body seemed transformed into an inhuman semblance. He meandered along the craggy trails seeking sustenance from the environment in which he pleasantly embraced. Squatting, gawking, loping forward, and repeating this ritual throughout the night.

As he sat catlike, staring into the misty, blustery night, a field mouse ran across a protruding rock in front of Yousef's roost. With lightning fast reflexes, he plucked the small rodent into his grasp. He played with the captured mouse, at first dropping it in his lap and waiting for the mouse to hastily make its retreat, only for Yousef to adroitly ensnare the small animal once again. At last he grew tired of his captive. He brought the small creature to his bared teeth, where he swiftly bit into the fury bundle and devoured the animal whole.

CHAPTER 72

SPECIAL AGENT GARZA and Sharon Martinez returned to the FBI field office where they poured over every report of possible Yousef Khan sightings. This included wacky musings of a public out of control. With the latest attempted bombing at the Albuquerque airport leaked to the press, the media fanned the flames of possible scenarios, connections to foreign governments, and conspiracy theories.

"Tony listen to this one. This lady called into 911 to report that there were three foreign midgets in her back yard. The lady stated that the midgets were trying to make off with a statue of the Virgin Mary, and that the foreigners obviously targeted her because of her Christian upbringing. When the dispatcher asked her how she knew the intruders were foreign, the lady replied, 'because of the funny clothes that they were wearing.'"

"We'll probably start getting some *Elvis* sightings next," laughed Tony.

"And look at all the reports on small guys riding blue bicycles, there must be thirty of them here," mused Sharon.

"That's what makes investigative work so interesting," Tony replied.

Working until after six P.M., Tony suggested to Sharon that they call it quits for the day. "He's still out there, and sooner or later we'll get the break we need to track him down. The BOLO we issued yesterday will eventually play out. He's got no transportation to speak of, other than a bike, and no where to hide."

"What if he steals a car—and makes his way to the border," asked Sharon.

"That's a possibility," injected Tony. "But for some reason I think he'll stay in the area."

"Gut feeling?" asked Sharon.

"You bet," Tony nodded.

CHAPTER 73

YOUSEF CONTINUED WITH his nightly habit of roaming the high mountain terrain. Sitting on his heels, he would scan the dark desert skyline. Listening for creatures of prey, he seemed at peace with himself. However, to a human observer he would appear more feral animal than a rational human male.

When he could not find or catch his victuals, he would return to the restaurant where he would devour large amounts of raw meat and other uncooked fare. On his third night, as he was climbing out from the restaurant's window, a night watchman almost encountered him as he leaped into the thick underbrush. After discovering the clutter in the kitchen, the watchman believed a wild beast had broken into the building. As it turns out the guard was not far off.

Yousef's clothes had become heavily soiled and ragged because of his nighttime excursions. His once clean shaven face had grown a dark bristle and mixed with the mud and other accumulated grime gave Yousef a vagrant appearance. Malodorous and unkempt, Yousef's manifestation into something deprived and uncultivated had taken place in a relatively short time span.

He no longer thought of his mission, his past, or his divine destiny. His consciousness now centered on mere subsistence, and being somehow connected with his natural, instinctive urges. He continued to sleep most of day and only ventured out during the nighttime hours. For hours at a time, he would stare unfocused into the night. He withdrew from his trancelike state only when he felt or heard movement from an animal or other living creature that he senses could discern.

CHAPTER 74

THE FOLLOWING DAY, Tony and Sharon returned to the Albuquerque field office where they continued the process of running down any possible lead. All calls and reports were meticulously logged and credible details were followed up by FBI task force personnel. This procedure was time consuming and dead ends often manifested varied degrees of frustration.

"We don't seem to be accomplishing anything," complained Sharon.

"I know, Shar—just hang in there. Sooner or later we'll get the right information that will lead to something. Persistence, persistence, persistence—tempered by keen judgment, sound investigative technique, novel powers of observation, and all this followed by downright good-luck."

"Okay," smiled Sharon.

By middle afternoon Tony walked over to the desk where Sharon was busy scrutinizing various documents. "I need a break," stated Tony, "let's split for some chow."

"Where do you want to eat, Tony?"

"Let's try something different, how 'bout *Murphy's Mule Barn?*"

"What?" asked Sharon.

"You'll see," laughed Tony.

Tony drove along Alameda boulevard and took a left at 2nd street. Arriving at the nondescript restaurant, Sharon did not know what to think. A friendly waitress escorted them to their table. "We don't need menus; we're both having the 'chicken fried steak,'" volunteered Tony.

"Where do you come up with these places?" asked a grinning Sharon.

"Occupational hazard," laughed Tony.

Returning to the office an hour later and noticing a new report, Tony hollered, "hey guys, we might have something here!"

Sharon hurried over to Tony's desk, "what have you got?"

"A tram employee just reported to APD that he found an abandoned mountain bike, in great condition, lying in a ditch off of Tramway road. And—oh by the way, the color is bright blue."

CHAPTER 75

WITHIN THIRTY MINUTES, Tony and Sharon arrived at the site of the abandoned bicycle listed in the police report. Two Albuquerque police cruisers were parked along the side of the road. As Tony got out of his vehicle, three APD officers strolled over. "The bike is over this way," one of the patrolman pointed and escorted Tony to a drainage ditch.

"It could be Khan's bike," remarked Tony, "I'm going to call our forensics guys out and see if we can get a match with Khan's DNA recovered from his residence. Any chance you guys can get a canine search team out here?"

"APD doesn't have any dog SAR teams, but we might be able to locate a team somewhere else in the community. We'll call it in, and see what we can come up with," replied one of the officers.

"In the mean time, we'll stay out here to guard the bike until your crime scene guys show up."

"Thanks," said Tony and got back into his Suburban with Sharon in tow.

"Do you think it's his bike, Tony?" asked Sharon.

"No way to tell for sure until our crime techs can verify—we'll see what they can come up with."

Sharon and Tony returned to the field office and nervously hung out awaiting some news. Two hours later APD phoned and relayed to Tony that they had located a K9 Search & Recue team in Los Alamos. "They're a civilian volunteer team, and they won't be able to make it down here till daybreak tomorrow," mentioned the officer.

"By then hopefully we can verify if it is in fact Khan's bike. Thanks," said Tony hanging up the phone.

Three and half hours went by until Tony received the call he was waiting on. "Tony, this is Mitch. We got a fingerprint match on the bike that matches one taken a few days ago in Khan's home."

"Great work, Mitch," exclaimed Tony.

Garza called the APD dispatcher, "We're going need those K9s tomorrow. Please let me know what time that we can rendezvous, and what they need to sniff from Khan's personal effects?"

"I'll get back to ya," replied the dispatcher.

CHAPTER 76

SPECIAL AGENT GARZA and Sharon Martinez woke early in an effort to meet with the K9 search and rescue volunteers. Before he retired to his townhouse the day before, Garza stopped by the former residence of Yousef Khan. He needed to obtain a personal item of clothing or some article that had retained Khan's scent. Since the residence was relatively barren, Garza had a harder time than expected selecting an appropriate garment or other article which would fulfill the requirement. Finally Garza chose a worn tee-shirt that he found in Khan's closet.

Garza told Sharon to dress down and wear comfortable attire. He prepped her that the day would most likely be physically demanding with searing heat, treacherous walking conditions, along with insects and other critters.

Sharon emerged from her bedroom wearing blue jeans, tennis shoes, and an oversized sweatshirt. Smiling from the kitchen, Tony remarked, "the dangly earrings are a good touch Shar."

"Well you never know what we are likely to encounter," Sharon grinned, "I have to be prepared."

"Just so you know," said Tony, "you look nice in whatever you're wearing."

"Thanks Tony, I really appreciate that."

"I just didn't want you to think that I'm some sort of..... well I mean I didn't want you to think I was hitting on you or something."

"Again Tony, I appreciate the comment," said Sharon. "And no, I wouldn't think that about you. I just want you to be yourself around me. Don't be so guarded. You won't offend me, I'm a big girl, and I can take care of myself."

"Okay then," replied Tony. "We better get moving."

"I'm ready, whenever you are," said Sharon good-naturedly.

At a little before six in the morning, Tony and Sharon sat in the car listening to the radio awaiting the arrival of the K9 team. Twenty minutes later Tony could see headlights approaching slowly from the deserted roadway.

"I think they're here," muttered Tony.

A late model pickup slowly pulled up and parked next to Tony's vehicle. Two darkened figures got out of the cab and ambled toward the parked SUV. Tony emerged from his government vehicle.

"Special Agent Garza?" a tall, lean middle-aged man asked.

"Yep, that's me," replied Garza as he extended his hand.

"I'm Jon Wilkens, and this is Bob Frence."

"Thanks for coming guys" intoned Garza. "And this is Sharon Martinez with the Department of Homeland Security."

"Hello ma'am," replied both men.

The taller man walked to the rear bed of the pickup. "And this is Rex, and Job," announced the man as he looked at two dogs reclining in the truck bed.

Both dogs appeared half-asleep. Rex was a large, black and brown German shepherd, and Job was a lean, fawn colored Weimaraner. "Let's wait until first light, and then we'll head out," stated Jon.

CHAPTER 77

At 6:38 THE sun was finally breaking over the mountains toward the East. "Up Job," commanded Jon.

The dog jumped from the bed of the truck and stood alert on the right side of the handler. "Agent Garza, could you hand me the tee-shirt?" asked Jon.

After SA Garza handed over the garment, Jon tore the shirt into two halves.

"What did you do that for?" asked Tony.

"One half for Job who is a scent dog, and the other half for Rex who is a tracking dog," explained Jon.

"What's the difference?" asked Tony.

"Job has been trained to pick up the scent of a subject from the air. With his extraordinary nose, he will process scent signals to find the subject that are carried in the wind. Bob's dog Rex is a tracking/trailing dog. Rex is trained to follow the specific scent left behind by the missing subject and hopefully follow that smell right to the missing person."

"Clear as mud," said Tony shaking his head.

"At any rate, Rex is going to take the lead, and Job and I will follow," advised Jon.

"Where do you want us," asked Tony.

"Just try to keep up," grinned Jon.

"Go," Bob commanded, and Rex scurried up the trail.

The other dog quickly followed with Tony and Sharon hurrying to keep up. Twenty yards up the steep path, both handlers stopped abruptly.

"He's alerted on something," shouted Bob.

Seconds later Tony and Sharon watched as Jon held his dog by his side. Bob was rewarding Rex with a treat, as the dog stared—fixated on a red "lobo's" ball cap.

"Good job," declared Tony. "This is going to be easier than I thought."

CHAPTER 78

TWO HOURS LATER the dog handlers along with their two dogs had barely made the halfway point up the precipitous mountain trail. Tony and Sharon followed the handlers but Sharon in particular labored. She was starting to fall back several yards behind the group. Tony waited along the steep pathway and in a cajoling voice announced, "come on Sharon, you can make it."

"I really don't know, Tony, I'm starting to feel faint and my legs are so tired—I just don't know if I can continue."

Tony raced ahead to inform the dog handlers to continue and that he was hanging back with Sharon at a slower pace. Tony returned to Sharon's side voicing encouragement to push on. "At this point Sharon, just be safe and take your time—I'll be right behind you."

"Okay Tony, I'm sorry to slow you down," muttered an exasperated Sharon.

"Slow and steady," encouraged Tony.

The vertical stony pathway was littered with tremendous granite boulders. Limestone rock formations cut along the rugged mountain face, with gnarled pine trees growing out of voids and creases in the most unlikely conditions. Although, the setting was majestic and miraculously beautiful, Sharon was too drained to appreciate the view. Somehow she soldiered onward and upward as Tony shouted words of encouragement.

By early afternoon Sharon, with Tony at her side emerged onto a clearing at the peak of the mountain. Exhausted, Sharon labored over to a rustic wooden bench crafted from a tree stump. She sat, nursing her feet. Tony strolled over to the handlers who were draining bottles of water into the open mouths of their canines.

"Find anything?" asked Tony, addressing the two men.

"Nope," replied Bob. "Job alerted a few times, but we didn't find anything. We are getting ready to go down the back side and see if we pick up anything. If you could get someone to pick us up and take us back to our pickup in a couple hours, we'd be appreciative."

"Not a problem," said Tony. "The lady needs to rest a spell, so I'll stay here with her and get a lift for us too. If you happen to encounter anything, I'll give you my cell number."

"You bet," replied Bob.

"How are ya doing, Shar?" Tony asked, as he took a seat beside her on the rustic bench.

"I'm starting to get my wind back, but legs are spent. I'm sorry Tony."

"Nothing to be sorry for Shar, we just started off at too fast a pace. Anyway, the dogs didn't find anything. Bob and Jon have taken the dogs down the backside, and I've called my office to pick them up in a couple of hours. As soon you're up to it, let's wander over to the restaurant and grab some chow," Tony said, as he pointed to a building in the distance.

CHAPTER 79

SHARON AND TONY ordered from the *High Finance Restaurant's* lunch menu as Sharon recovered from the morning's excruciating excursion.

"So what happens now?" asked Sharon.

"Well we know he's around here, or has been here. The dogs alerted along some of the paths but the handlers didn't find anything. They mentioned that the heavy rains might have diminished some of the scent. So we'll see, let's enjoy our lunch and see what develops."

Drinking her second glass of water, Sharon added, "okay."

Finishing their late lunch of chicken quesadillas and steak and green chili nachos, the restaurant manager stopped by and asked, "How were your meals, folks?"

"Great," said Tony.

"Are you folks just traveling though?" the friendly manager inquired.

"In a manner of speaking," smiled Tony. "I'm with the FBI and Ms. Martinez is with the Department of Homeland Security. Actually we are working on a case. We think a suspect is holding up somewhere in the area."

"That's interesting," responded the manager. "Actually we've had a couple of break-ins this week, and we can't figure out how or why."

"What did they take?" Tony asked curiously.

"That's what perplexing," responded the manager. "We haven't noticed anything of value taken, however some meat and vegetables are missing, and food products have littered our kitchen preparation area. We have a roving patrol during the night, and one of the guards thought he saw a large animal jumping into the vegetation outside. But we can't find out how this man or animal is able to get into the building."

"Interesting," mused Tony.

A short time later, another agent from the field office arrived, and gave Tony and Sharon a ride back to Tony's government vehicle which he left parked on the other side of the mountain. Jon and Bob were finishing up loading their truck when Tony approached them.

"Any luck guys?"

"Nope," nodded Jon. "Not a thing on the far side, but like we told you, we got some 'hits' on the trail going up. And definitely the red hat belongs to the missing guy."

"Well don't worry," said Tony, "if he's up there, we'll get him. And again, thanks so much for all your hard work, and the dog's hard work too."

"It has been a pleasure, hope the lady is feeling better," said Jon, as they drove away.

Chapter 80

Back at Tony's townhouse, Sharon was taking a shower while Tony grilled salmon on his patio grill. When Sharon joined him a few minutes later, Tony asked, "Ready for a 'cerveza' Shar?"

"You bet, Tony!"

Relaxing on a patio recliner, Sharon made an observation. "You know Tony, I'm certainly impressed that you can unwind the way you do. A radical terrorist is on the loose out there, and you are able to enjoy a beer and make dinner. All the ups-and-downs during the last few days and you are able to let-it-go, seemingly at will."

"Truth be told, Sharon, I have never been able totally let-it-go. But since my divorce, I've realized I've had to make adjustments in my life. Introspection has never been my strong suit, but I've learned over the years that I needed to be able take control over things I could manage and let go of things beyond my control. So, rather than letting a case consume me, I've been able to put it into the proper perspective. Anyway it allows me to better 'process' information, and act in more rational manner when needed. Same with this investigation, Khan is never totally out of my mind, but I've taught myself that sooner or later he's going to slip up, and we'll be there to put the cuffs on him."

"Do you really think that he's going to slip up?" asked Sharon.

"You bet! We've already got him on the run, and were getting close. I really think he's still in the area, and when the time is right, we'll get him."

"Tony, do you believe in destiny?" inquired Sharon.

"Boy is this conversation getting a little deep?" considered Tony.

"I mean," explained Sharon, "that some things are just meant to happen. You know, like good and evil. Evil raises its ugly self, then good triumphs over the bad. History gives us a multitude of examples where a person, a nation, or a situation evolves that sets the world in a tailspin—then a series of events takes place that eventually corrects those circumstances."

"Sharon, I think you're ready for another beer," laughed Tony.

"Oh, okay Tony. Lets eat!"

CHAPTER 81

RISING EARLY, TONY went for a long run along Albuquerque's west mesa. He thought about his day ahead and how he would proceed. He also contemplated what the *High Finance Restaurant* manager happened to mention during his and Sharon's late afternoon lunch the day before. He was convinced the restaurant's late night thefts were connected to Yousef Khan. The circumstances were too convenient for Tony to ignore.

Meanwhile, Sharon was getting ready to travel to her Santa Fe office where she planned to brief her boss on the events that had transpired during the last few days.

Tony had returned from his jog just as Sharon was getting into her car. "Have a good run, Tony?"

Tony, sweating profusely replied, "You bet, a good run helps clear my head. Are you planning on coming back this evening?"

"Yeah Tony, if it's alright—I should be back sometime in the late afternoon."

"Great, you're my barometer," quipped Tony.

"A barometer," rejoined Sharon, "what's that suppose to mean?"

"I just mean you help me see things in this case, that I might miss otherwise—you keep me grounded in reality."

"Okay, I'm your 'grounded barometer?'"

"You know what I'm saying," grinned Tony.

Sharon smiled, "What's your plan for today?"

"Well, after I wash some of this stink off me, I'm planning on making a return trip to see the manager at the restaurant where we had lunch yesterday."

"See ya later Tony."

"Drive safe Shar."

"You too Tony, and be careful up there."

Tony was showered and was on the road in less than forty minutes. One hour and forty-five minutes later he pulled into the restaurant parking lot where the manager was waiting for him.

"We had another break-in last night," an excited manager exclaimed.

"Let me take a look," suggested Tony.

The manager led Tony into a side door leading into the kitchen. Tony noticed food droppings, on the floor next to a large stainless steel refrigerator. "Mind if I take a look around?" asked Tony.

"Be my guest," replied the manager.

Tony went back outside and slowly walked the perimeter of the restaurant. Carefully examining the building's foundation, windows, and doors, Tony stopped abruptly along the side of a narrow walkway. "Look at this," said Tony as he pointed to a window."

"I don't see anything," whispered the manager.

"The window screen has been creased back, and it looks like recent damage," suggested Tony.

"I'll get one of our maintenance folks to get this secured immediately," shouted the manager.

"No leave it alone!" demanded Tony, a plan formulating in his mind.

Chapter 82

Tony had a brief discussion with the restaurant manager before departing for his Albuquerque field office. Arriving at his office a short time later, Tony was met by one of the surveillance support technicians.

"What I need," said Tony "is a small camera that can see in the dark, and a remote monitor that can be set up in my vehicle."

"Got it!" said the technician, "Where do you want it installed?"

"At the *High Finance Restaurant*," exclaimed Tony. "The manager is waiting for you now, and I have to have this ready to roll before tomorrow night."

"Shouldn't be a problem," beamed the technician.

Entering his front door, Tony found Sharon busy chopping vegetables on his kitchen counter. "What's for dinner Sharon—smells good?"

"Fatatas!" shouted Sharon.

"Yum sounds tasty!" murmured Tony.

Following a leisurely meal, Tony announced, "We need to sleep-in tomorrow, Sharon, how 'bout we stay up late tonight and watch a movie?"

"Why are we sleeping in, Tony?"

"I or I should say, 'we' are going to stake-out the restaurant we ate at yesterday—sometime after nightfall, late tomorrow night."

"How do we know Khan will return?" asked Sharon.

"Well," answered Tony, "he broke-in again last night, and I'll bet the restaurant is Khan's main source of food."

"Okay Tony, so what movie do you have in mind?"

"How about *TheBridge on the River Kwai*? Have you ever seen it? It's actually one of my all time favorites".

"I've never heard of it," declared Sharon. "But I'm game."

CHAPTER 83

DESPITE NOT GETTING to sleep until after 2:00 PM, Tony awoke just after 7:00 AM. Today he decided to run along the Rio Grande river trail. The sun was just starting to rise above the mountains to the east, and the dense growth of cottonwood trees along the trail provided a tranquil setting for Tony to run and enjoy the warm autumn day. The river's slow-flowing current supplied a soft, almost muted, water feature to his endeavor. Tony loved this time in the morning.

Tony ran and ran. Feeling especially energized on this peaceful morning he ran some more—eventually logging in more than fourteen miles. This was not a typical run for Tony as his customary run was between three to five miles. Arriving back home just before 10:00, it appeared that Sharon was still in bed. Tony enjoyed a soothing shower and dressed into a polo-shirt and worn blue jeans. When Tony emerged from his bedroom, Sharon was in the kitchen preparing breakfast, still attired in her nightgown.

"I thought you said to sleep in late?" asked Sharon.

"I did," responded Tony. "I didn't get up till seven."

"Well aren't you going to have a hard time staying awake tonight?"

Tony smiled, "No I'll be fine, just you wait and see."

After a filling brunch of huevos rancheros, fried potatoes, and guacamole, Tony discussed his day ahead. "First I need to go into the office where my guys are going to equip my vehicle with a night vision monitor. Then I'll come back here and we can relax for a few hours before we head out late tonight. Anything you need to do today Shar?"

"Nothing special, while you're at your office, I think I'll go for a jog. After our mountain tracking expedition, it made me realize how out of shape I am."

"Take it slow and easy," advised Tony.

CHAPTER 84

ARRIVING AT HIS office a few minutes later, Tony met with a very animated support technician. "Look Tony, I was able to get my hands on a state-of-the-art, second generation, STRU device. This beauty has infrared night-vision illumination, over 550 lines of resolution, a signal to noise ratio of 50Db, and a 50 millimeter bullet lens."

"That's really great Sean, but all that I need is to know where the on and off switch is," laughed Tony. "Did you have any trouble with the installation at the restaurant?"

"No trouble at all," replied the technician. "I got the camera pointing right at the window you told me about, and it should work great, but remember the monitor in your vehicle has to be within twenty yards of the camera. Will that be a problem Tony?"

"Should work out just fine," said Tony. "I just need to park far enough away so we don't scare off the perp. You got anything else for me?"

"No," reply Sean. "Just keep me in mind for your next install. The manager at the restaurant gave me a free lunch after I finished. I think he was impressed with our team."

"That's great," said Tony. "I better get back and get some rest; it's going to be a long night."

"So long Tony and good luck tonight."

"Thanks Sean, I can use all the luck I can get."

Tony returned to his townhouse where he found Sharon fresh from a shower.

"How was your run Shar?"

"Great now that I'm done. I really need to get myself in better shape."

"Just work it slow and steady," advised Tony.

CHAPTER 85

DURING THE LAST couple of days, Yousef Khan's psychological state had deteriorated steadily. Waking inside his small cavern during the nighttime hours, he would scrounge for sustenance wherever he could find it. This usually meant a handful of pine nuts or insects crawling about. Later into the hours of darkness, if his hunger was not sufficiently satisfied he would return to the mountaintop restaurant for additional nourishment.

After filling his stomach, he would scamper about the mountain paths often creeping through prickly vegetation and harsh underbrush. During these excursions, the exposed parts of his body endured numerous surface cuts and abrasions. His face and arms were now crisscrossed with purplish welts and pus-filled scabs. Yousef's appearance took on the look of an itinerant who lost a brawl with a feral feline.

Yousef often soiled himself not cognizant that the stench from his secretions was emanating from his own body. When Yousef heard a howling lobo, or the bay or shriek of another animal—he would follow the sound to seek out its source. Too labored in his saunter, and telegraphing his presence with his foul odor, he was never able to get close to the beast which he sought out. But he continued to wander throughout the darkness returning to his surreptitious stony fissure before sunrise.

Two nights earlier, a fawn-colored mountain lion sat on an elevated rocky perch and watched, as Yousef drifted along a rock-strewn trail below. Yousef somehow sensed the cougar's presence, but was unable to visually locate the predator in the darkness. As he made his way back to his cave, the mountain lion leisurely followed. As dawn approached, Yousef lay upon his bed of pine straw and closed his eyes. The cougar issued a deafening roar, and then retreated from Yousef's nesting region.

CHAPTER 86

TONY AND SHARON drove leisurely toward *The High Finance Restaurant* on the eastern side of the Sandia's. Because the majority of the restaurant personnel would not vacate the building until the last tram ride back to the city, Tony estimated the break-ins occurred sometime after midnight. So he planned to be parked, semi-hidden alongside the frontage road approaching the rear of the eatery just before the last employee departed. Sharon had packed a large bag of sandwiches, snacks, and soft drinks. Once in place, Tony turned on the wireless camera monitor, and received good image feeds from the camera. The camera's night vision feature allowed Tony and Sharon to view the interior window along with most of the supporting wall where the suspected intrusion occurred.

"So Tony, what happens now?"

"We wait," whispered Tony.

Shortly after 2:00 A.M., Sharon muttered, "Tony this is getting spooky—sitting here, all alone in the dark!"

"You're not alone, I'm here."

"You know what I mean, Tony. It's just that it's so dark—and eerily silent."

"You want to tell ghost stories Shar?" mused Tony.

Tony sat up abruptly, "look, we got something on the screen."

Hastily Sharon sat straight up in her seat, brushing her head against the dashboard, "what do we do now?"

"We wait until he gets into the restaurant, then we go block his exit. We'll have him trapped."

"Now!" clamored Tony. "Be careful and follow me."

CHAPTER 87

CAUTIOUSLY TONY CREPT to the side of the building laboring to keep his footing along the narrow passageway. Moments later Sharon approached, "Shhh—stay down," whispered Tony.

Tony could barely make out a shadowy figure inside the darkened restaurant. Breathing rapidly in anticipation of the ultimate confrontation, Tony tried to steady his nerves and remain silent. Sharon remained behind Tony and also kept mute. A rubbing, sliding din was scarcely audible on the other side of the window. Suddenly a silhouette appeared pushing outward on the window screen. Yousef Khan slid quietly through the opening. Once his feet touched ground, Tony turned on his Maglite illuminating the view.

"FBI, put your hands in the air!" shouted Tony.

The harried figure seemed to comply with the harsh command—then abruptly darted around Tony, and raced down the sloping pathway. Tony quickly followed, trying desperately to overtake the diminutive form. As Tony pursued the fleeing profile, Yousef would dodge right and left in a panicked desperation. Moments later the trail ended, leaving Yousef enclosed between a sheer rock face on one side and the darkness of the empty valley below.

"Alright Yousef, you have no where to go. Put you hands over your head."

Yousef peered into the eyes of his pursuer, his gaze steady and unblinking. Crossing his arms over his upper torso—fingers pointed outward, Yousef shifted his head toward the full moon. He then erupted with an implausible howl, diving head-first, into the murky valley below.

The FBI agent stood stunned with Sharon coming up at his rear. Completely shocked at what they had just witnessed, Sharon shook her head in disbelief.

Finally Tony whispered, "God's will, little Joe."

Epilogue

YOUSEF KHAN'S BADLY mangled body was recovered several hours later with the help of a local Search and Rescue helicopter team from Kirtland Air Force Base. Following an autopsy, Khan's body was transported back to his native Pakistan and interred.

The ten captured Pakistani students are currently being held in a high-risk, federal detention facility. All ten are being charged with domestic terrorism under the provisions of Title 18 of the U. S. Code. At the advice of their defense lawyer, all are pleading "not guilty."

Imam Saadi is currently being held without bail and is under indictment for harboring fugitives along with a number of related charges. His attorney is claiming that his client is mentally incompetent to stand trial.

The Glenwood Hills engineer escaped prosecution, however subsequently lost his position with Sandia National Laboratories due to security violations. He is running for city council in the next Albuquerque election.

Special Agent Garza was offered a promotion to Supervisory Special Agent at the FBI Washington Field Office (WFO). Garza declined, stating he was content with his present position.

Sharon Martinez received a "citation for merit" from Headquarters, Department of Homeland Security. Sharon has also applied for a vacant "intelligence analyst" position at the FBI Field Office in Albuquerque. Tony maintains that Sharon is a "shoo-in" and should be receiving an offer soon.

And oh, Sharon and Tony's close friends now refer to them as "an item."

FINIS